THE TRUMP PRESIDENCY

John Allen

San Diego, CA

© 2020 ReferencePoint Press, Inc.
Printed in the United States

For more information, contact:
ReferencePoint Press, Inc.
PO Box 27779
San Diego, CA 92198
www.ReferencePointPress.com

ALL RIGHTS RESERVED.
No part of this work covered by the copyright hereon may be reproduced or used in any form or by any means—graphic, electronic, or mechanical, including photocopying, recording, taping, web distribution, or information storage retrieval systems—without the written permission of the publisher.

LIBRARY OF CONGRESS CATALOGING-IN-PUBLICATION DATA

Name: Allen, John, 1957– author.
Title: The Trump Presidency/By John Allen.
Description: San Diego, CA: ReferencePoint Press, Inc. 2020. | Includes
  bibliographical references and index.
Identifiers: LCCN 2019029105 (print) | LCCN 2019029106 (ebook) | ISBN
  9781682827598 (library binding) | ISBN 9781682827604 (ebook)
Subjects: LCSH: Trump, Donald, 1946—Juvenile literature. |
  Presidents—United States—Juvenile literature. | United
  States—Politics and government—2016–
Classification: LCC E912 .A42 2020 (print) | LCC E912 (ebook) | DDC
  973.933092—dc23
LC record available at https://lccn.loc.gov/2019029105
LC ebook record available at https://lccn.loc.gov/2019029106

CONTENTS

Introduction   4
A President Like No Other

Chapter One   8
A Combative Style

Chapter Two   20
Reversing Course in Foreign Policy

Chapter Three   32
Illegal Immigration and Building the Wall

Chapter Four   44
Tax Cuts and Tariffs for the Economy

Chapter Five   56
Controversy on the Environment

Source Notes   67
For Further Research   72
Index   74
Picture Credits   79
About the Author   80

INTRODUCTION

A President Like No Other

In April 2019, a month after roundups of undocumented immigrants at the Mexican border reached a twelve-year high, President Donald J. Trump suggested a new policy. He said he was considering a plan to send immigrants arriving at the border to so-called sanctuary cities. These are cities that have designated themselves as safe havens for undocumented immigrants, offering protection from federal efforts to arrest them. "Due to the fact that Democrats are unwilling to change our very dangerous immigration laws, we are indeed, as reported, giving strong considerations to placing illegal immigrants in Sanctuary Cities only,"[1] Trump wrote on Twitter. The president's announcement was typical of his approach to divisive issues. He was announcing a plan that seemed designed to infuriate his political foes at the same time it pretended to solve a timely crisis. Love him or hate him—and few Americans remain neutral on Trump—he has established himself as a president unlike any other in US history.

A Billionaire Celebrity

Trump's rise to the White House has unfolded in full view of the American public. High-profile business deals first brought him to national attention several decades ago. Born in 1946, Trump was still in his twenties when his father groomed him to take over the family real estate business in New York. In 1971 Trump became company president, renaming it the Trump Organization.

He proceeded to broker deals and develop projects that helped reshape the Manhattan skyline. Trump Tower, a fifty-eight-story Fifth Avenue skyscraper with gold-plated furnishings and decor and a huge glass atrium, stands as a monument to his flashy lifestyle. Trump went on to develop hotels, casinos, and golf courses worldwide and manage beauty pageants and modeling agencies. His Trump brand of products and services continues to rake in millions.

There were many setbacks and controversies along the way. These included six bankruptcies of hotel and casino properties, and a real-estate school, called Trump University, had to shut down due to lawsuits for fraud. Yet Trump's reputation as a tough and savvy businessperson grew. It eventually led to his role in the reality TV show *The Apprentice*, on which he would dispatch losing contestants with a terse "You're fired!" Trump the billionaire celebrity also became known for glamorous wives and extramarital affairs that kept the gossip columnists buzzing.

A Stunning Election Night

With his habit of speaking his mind on virtually any topic, it was no surprise when Trump turned to politics. When he announced his run for the White House in 2015 with the slogan Make America Great Again, almost no one gave him any chance of success. On the campaign trail, he trashed his opponents in the large Republican field, giving them disparaging nicknames like "Little Marco" Rubio and "Lyin' Ted" Cruz. He concentrated on a few issues, such as illegal immigration and tariffs on imports to protect American jobs. He promised to "drain the swamp" in Washington, DC, by limiting the influence of lobbyists and other political insiders. He also told frequent lies and half-truths and was accused of racism in his appeals to white voters in Middle America. Yet despite his brash style and the condemnation of many on the left and right, Trump swept to the Republican nomination.

In the general election, pollsters overwhelmingly predicted Trump would lose to his Democratic opponent, Hillary Clinton.

President Donald J. Trump speaks to news reporters in the White House Rose Garden in 2019. Few Americans are neutral when it comes to how they view the nation's forty-fifth president.

Election Night, however, revealed that support for Trump had surged in the final week. Although Clinton won the popular vote by nearly 3 million votes, Trump secured a narrow victory in electoral votes. His shocking triumph left pundits and commentators dumbfounded, with some elated at the results and others in tears at the prospect of a Trump presidency. The next day many leading columnists forecast disaster for the nation. "So we are very probably looking at a global recession, with no end in sight," wrote Nobel Prize–winning economist Paul Krugman in the *New York Times*. "I suppose we could get lucky somehow. But on economics, as on everything else, a terrible thing has just happened."[2]

> "So we are very probably looking at a global recession, with no end in sight. . . . On economics, as on everything else, a terrible thing has just happened."[2]
>
> —*New York Times* columnist Paul Krugman on Trump's election as president

Chaos and Accomplishment

From the beginning Trump's presidency has been marked by combativeness and chaos. Washington insiders, including most of the media, Democrats, and so-called Never Trump Republicans, despised the new president. His opponents charged him with racism, sexism, Islamophobia, and even treason. Trump responded with a blizzard of tweets on every conceivable topic, including jabs at his political foes and critics in the media. He labeled stories that criticized him as "fake news" and even branded the national media as "the true Enemy of the People."[3]

Trump's cabinet and staff appointments have included several well-respected Washington veterans, but his unpredictable temperament has led to a series of firings and resignations. Leaked reports claim the White House atmosphere is chaotic, with Trump liable to change his mind about policy from day to day. More cabinet-level officials have left his administration in its first two years than in the first four years of either of the last two presidencies.

Despite the turmoil and missteps, Trump has also presided over solid accomplishments. Far from collapsing, the US economy under Trump has seen strong growth and rising employment. In foreign affairs, Trump has questioned old alliances and antagonized some allies. But he has also ordered successful military strikes against terrorist groups in the Middle East, slapped tough sanctions on Russia and Iran, and confronted China over unfair trade practices. The two new justices he nominated for the Supreme Court have pleased conservatives with their commitment to the Constitution's original meaning.

> "President Trump is a disrupter. And I felt politics needed some disruption."[4]
>
> —Ted Baker, a Trump voter in Muncie, Indiana

With his boasts, taunts, and impulsive behavior, Trump will always be a divisive president. Yet for his supporters, what matters are Trump's results. "President Trump is a disrupter," says Ted Baker, a Trump voter in Muncie, Indiana. "And I felt politics needed some disruption. Now disruption's never easy. But it is important."[4]

CHAPTER ONE

A Combative Style

In the November 2018 midterm elections, American voters delivered a blow to the Trump administration, switching control of the House of Representatives from Republicans to Democrats. With committee chairs changing hands, Democrats now promised to conduct far-reaching investigations of Trump, from his alleged collusion with Russia in the 2016 election to his tax returns and business dealings prior to (and after) becoming president. The day after the midterms, Trump addressed a White House news conference in his usual combative style. Despite loss of the House, he pointed to Republican gains in the Senate and characterized the election as close to a total victory. He mocked Republicans who had rejected his support on the campaign trail—and lost. He called a CNN reporter "a rude, terrible person."[5] When asked if his embrace of the label "nationalist" encouraged white supremacist groups, he attacked the reporter for asking what he called a racist question. He warned that if House Democrats insisted on investigating him, "then we're going to do the same thing [to them], then government comes to a halt and I blame them."[6] Clearly, Trump had no intention of admitting defeat. His aggressive response to the election setback was typical of his governing approach from the start.

Wading into Controversy

Trump seems to delight in baiting his critics and wading into controversy. His campaign slogan, Make America Great Again—shortened to MAGA on his supporters' bright red ball caps—

was a deliberate jab at former president Barack Obama and the Democrats. Trump felt they had weakened the United States and that it was his job to restore the nation's military and economic might.

As a presidential candidate, Trump made headlines daily with his campaign speeches and pointed remarks to the media. His statements were either refreshingly candid or outrageously mean-spirited, depending on his listeners' viewpoint. He referred to immigrants from Mexico and Latin America as criminals, rapists, and drug dealers. He blasted longtime allies in Europe for not spending more on North Atlantic Treaty Organization (NATO) defenses. He vowed to scrap trade agreements in favor of new ones more favorable to America. Above all, he promised a new era of success and prosperity. "We're going to win. We're going to win so much," he told supporters at a May 2016 rally in Billings, Montana. "We're going to win at trade, we're going to win at the border. We're going to win so much, you're going to be so sick and tired of winning."[7]

Many times Trump seemed to cross the line with a reckless comment, leading to predictions that his campaign was finished. For example, in July 2015 he lashed out at Senator John McCain. As a US Navy pilot in the Vietnam War, McCain had been shot down, taken prisoner, and tortured by the North Vietnamese. Of McCain, one of Trump's most outspoken Republican critics, Trump said, "He's not a war hero. He's a war hero because he was captured. I like people that weren't captured."[8] Critics were outraged that Trump, who had avoided military service, would attack a highly decorated former prisoner of war. Yet somehow Trump survived the controversy. Opinion writers like CNN's Chris Cillizza saw this as a startling change in American politics—and not one for the better:

> "We're going to win at trade, we're going to win at the border. We're going to win so much, you're going to be so sick and tired of winning."[7]
>
> —Trump speaking at a 2016 rally in Billings, Montana

Everyone who knew anything assumed that attacking McCain's five years spent as a prisoner of war in Vietnam—a time that left the Arizona Republican with lifelong wounds—was a death sentence of Trump's political ambitions. . . . Except it didn't destroy Trump. For all the hand-wringing and predictions of doom for his campaign, he just kept right on going—first to the Republican presidential nomination and then to the White House. For many of his supporters, Trump's broadsides against McCain were music to their ears—finally someone was standing up to the political establishment in Washington! . . . But what Trump's comments about McCain should remind us of is this: Whether there is political gain to be found in dishonoring a lifelong public servant, it is simply wrong. It is not who we are—or who we should be.[9]

Aggressiveness and False Claims

Any thoughts that Trump might soften his rhetoric as president were soon dashed. If anything, he has been more combative in office than on the campaign trail. He relentlessly promotes himself and trashes his enemies. He calls Democratic senator Bernie Sanders "Crazy Bernie" or "the Nutty Professor." Democratic senator Elizabeth Warren, who made headlines for claiming Native American heritage, is "Pocahontas." He has tried to bully federal judges, foreign leaders, corporate chief executive officers (CEOs), lawmakers in both parties, agency heads, and union bosses. He has blasted the *New York Times* as a failing enterprise and labeled Ann Coulter, a conservative critic, as a "wacky nut job."[10] Trump even attacked basketball superstar LeBron James after James criticized him during an interview on CNN.

> "But what Trump's comments about McCain should remind us of is this: Whether there is political gain to be found in dishonoring a lifelong public servant, it is simply wrong. It is not who we are—or who we should be."[9]
>
> —CNN opinion writer Chris Cillizza

Waving "Make America Great Again" signs, Trump supporters rally in Georgia in 2018. The president's campaign slogan states his view that America has become weak and needs to be restored to greatness.

Trump's aggressive self-promotion often includes false claims. He declares victory even when he falls short, and he blames setbacks on opponents' lies or cheating. As political analyst Peter Baker notes:

> In Mr. Trump's world, there is a fine line between victor and victim. The president often veers back and forth, eager to be seen by others as the former even as he sees himself as the latter. To Mr. Trump, winning is always the goal, whether it be in business, politics, policy or even investigations, but even when he is on top, he lapses into anger and resentment, convinced that he has been unfairly treated and determined to strike back.[11]

Controversy in Charlottesville

Trump's refusal to back down when challenged by critics often leads to more controversy. One episode early in Trump's presidency drew accusations of racism from Trump's opponents. In August 2017 neo-Nazi and white supremacist groups held a Unite the Right rally in Charlottesville, Virginia. The rally began as a protest against removal of a statue of Confederate general Robert E. Lee. However, the far-right groups were intent on spreading a message of hate, marching with torches and chanting racist and anti-Semitic slogans. Counterprotesters, including black-clad members of Antifa (for "antifascist"), gathered to oppose the racist marchers. Confrontation turned to violence, and one of the neo-Nazis ran his car into the crowd, killing a young female counterprotester. In his comments on the incident, Trump blamed both groups for the violence. He also said, "But you also had people that were very fine people on both sides." Even members of Trump's own party expressed outrage about his statement.

However, Trump partisans believe the president has been treated unfairly on Charlottesville. They point out that his remarks on "very fine people" were followed by this: "And I'm not talking about the Neo-Nazis and the White nationalists, because they should be condemned totally." Regardless, the Charlottesville incident continues to cloud his term in office. Former vice president Joe Biden, in announcing his run for the White House, pointed to Trump's words after Charlottesville as the defining moment of his presidency.

Quoted in James S. Robbins, "Trump's Charlottesville Comments Twisted by Joe Biden and the Media," *USA Today*, April 26, 2019. www.usatoday.com.

After the election, Trump claimed his margin of victory in the Electoral College was the largest ever, when actually it was modest by historical standards. He insisted his loss in the popular vote was due to millions of illegal ballots cast for Hillary Clinton, although neither he nor anyone else ever provided proof of this. He asserts that his economic plan has created the greatest turnaround in American history, although he inherited a growing economy from his Democratic predecessor. Trump also says immigration is harming America and foreigners are invading in large numbers, when government figures show foreign workers boost economic activity. He has called climate change a hoax and portrayed Democrats as radical socialists. When his claims are challenged, Trump simply moves on to another topic.

Fact-checkers at the *Washington Post* assert that Trump had made more than ten thousand false or misleading claims in office as of June 2019. Journalists try to correct the record, but some fear that repeating his misstatements only helps spread his message. As for Trump's loyal core of supporters, they love his aggressive rhetoric and are not fazed by his falsehoods. Some contend that what the media reports as lies are often political views on which people may disagree. At any rate, polls in the spring of 2019 showed Trump's approval ratings on the rise. His approval fluctuates from 45 percent to 50 percent—a fairly solid mark for such a divisive president.

The Twitter Habit

Another thing that exasperates Trump's opponents is his constant use of Twitter. For Trump, however, Twitter is an important weapon in his arsenal. He uses it to reach his audience directly, without media filters. His Twitter feed has more than 60 million followers, which is 45 million less than Barack Obama's. Trump is not bashful about tweeting, posting 2,227 tweets in 2017 and increasing the number to 2,843 in 2018. All that Twitter activity strikes Trump's critics as foolish and unpresidential. During the 2016 campaign Trump seemed to agree, tweeting, "Don't worry, I'll give it up after I'm president. We won't tweet anymore. I don't know. Not presidential."[12] Nonetheless, as with so many things, Trump changed his mind about Twitter.

He often begins tweeting early in the morning, promoting his agenda, attacking enemies, making jokes, and boasting about his record. On March 13, 2018, he even announced the firing of Secretary of State Rex Tillerson via Twitter. A typical tweet from

July 2018 laid into one of his favorite targets, the national media: "The Fake News Media is going CRAZY! They are totally unhinged and in many ways, after witnessing first hand the damage they do to so many innocent and decent people, I enjoy watching. In 7 years, when I am no longer in office, their ratings will dry up and they will be gone!"[13]

Trump's tweets often touch on whatever is in the news. In April 2019, when Notre Dame Cathedral in Paris, France, was in flames, Trump tweeted advice on how to put out the fire. (Paris firefighters rejected his suggestion.) According to the political website Politico, about half of Trump's tweets promote his own success while about a third rip into his adversaries.

Special Counsel Robert Mueller speaks publicly about the Russia investigation in 2019. He concluded that Russia interfered in the 2016 presidential election, but he left open the question of whether Trump had obstructed justice during the investigation.

The Mueller Investigation

Many of Trump's most combative tweets have been aimed at a special counsel investigation of his campaign and presidency. In the summer of 2016, US intelligence concluded that Russia was working to tilt the presidential election in Trump's favor. The FBI began looking into contacts between members of the Trump campaign and Russians close to the Kremlin. Authorities also were concerned about a dossier compiled by a former British agent named Christopher Steele. The Steele dossier alleged various ties between Trump and Russia and included damaging stories that, if true, could be used by Russian president Vladimir Putin as blackmail material against Trump. After the election, when FBI director James Comey refused to say publicly that Trump was not a subject of the FBI probes, Trump fired him. Comey's dismissal caused angry Democrats to accuse Trump of obstruction of justice. It also led to the appointment of former FBI director Robert Mueller as special counsel to investigate charges of collusion (or a conspiracy) between Trump and Russia. In effect, the president of the United States stood accused of treason.

Mueller's investigation lasted almost two years, issued twenty-eight hundred subpoenas, and executed nearly five hundred search warrants. Trump repeatedly vented his anger about the probe on Twitter, calling it a witch hunt and a political hit job. With each leak of new information, cable news hosts and opinion writers predicted that Trump would be forced from office. In the end Mueller's team indicted thirty-four people, among whom were five Trump associates and campaign members—including Michael Flynn, Trump's original national security advisor. Mueller's report concluded that the Russian government had engaged in numerous systematic efforts to interfere in the 2016 election. However, Mueller ultimately found there was insufficient evidence of any conspiracy with Russia. He chose to leave open the question of whether Trump had obstructed justice.

Not surprisingly, Trump claimed total vindication. He railed against the so-called deep state that had failed to bring him down.

Investigations in Congress and the FBI revealed that the Steele dossier was paid for by the Clinton campaign and the Democratic National Committee. Its claims were never verified, yet it was used to help secure surveillance on the Trump campaign. Illegal leaks by intelligence officials had fed the media frenzy about the Trump-Russia story. To Trump's devoted followers, and even to some of his detractors, the president's rants about fake news seemed justified in this case. "You know what was fake news? Most of the

The Trump-Ukraine Impeachment Inquiry

In September 2019 Trump became embroiled in another controversy that seemed to place his presidency in danger. A whistleblower complaint from a CIA agent posted in the White House claimed that Trump had pushed Ukraine to investigate Joe Biden, a Trump rival in the 2020 presidential race. The anonymous whistleblower charged that Trump, during a July 25 phone call with Ukrainian president Volodymyr Zelensky, had threatened to withhold aid from Ukraine unless Zelensky agreed to dig up dirt on Biden and his son Hunter, who had business dealings in Ukraine.

Amidst a media frenzy, the White House released a transcript-like summary of Trump's phone call. It showed that he had asked Zelensky for "a favor," had suggested that the Bidens be investigated, and had offered Justice Department assistance. To Trump's critics, the call was evidence that the president had abused his power to help his 2020 reelection. On September 24, 2019, House Speaker Nancy Pelosi announced a formal impeachment inquiry to decide if enough evidence exists to warrant writing up articles of impeachment.

Trump and his defenders insisted he had done nothing wrong. On October 8, 2019, the White House announced it would not cooperate with the House impeachment inquiry. An eight-page letter from the White House Counsel said the House's impeachment effort was an attempt to "overturn the results of the 2016 election and deprive the American people of the President they have freely chosen."

Nevertheless, on October 16, Senate Majority Leader Mitch McConnell told Republican senators to be ready for an impeachment trial in the coming weeks.

"Letter from White House Counsel Pat Cipollone to House Leaders," *Washington Post*, October 8, 2019. www.washingtonpost.com.

Russiagate story," says Matt Taibbi, a left-wing political writer. "There was no Trump-Russia conspiracy, that thing we just spent *three years* chasing."[14] White House spokesperson Hogan Gidley adds, "I'm not going to begrudge Donald Trump for defending himself against a witch hunt and a hoax that was proven to be so. He's a counterpuncher."[15]

> "You know what was fake news? Most of the Russiagate story. There was no Trump-Russia conspiracy, that thing we just spent *three years* chasing."[14]
>
> —Matt Taibbi, political analyst for *Rolling Stone*

Chaos and Turnover

Due in part to Trump's combativeness, his administration has become a revolving door for everyone from cabinet officials to staff members. The president's tendency to act on impulse and emotion, along with his offhand management style, serves to create an atmosphere of chaos in the White House. According to former aide Cliff Sims, Trump often seems to thrive on conflict. "I've heard it said that every president gets the White House that they deserve," says Sims, "and I do think that some of the way that he operates, the creative chaos . . . kind of freewheeling style, his penchant for putting two rival staff members in a room and letting them fight it out over an issue does breathe some of this competitive aspect."[16]

Whatever the reason, turnover in the Trump cabinet has been historically high. By mid-January 2019, only two years into his term, Trump's cabinet had already seen twelve changes of staff. By the third year of the previous six presidencies combined, only sixteen people had left their cabinet jobs. Usually departures only begin in earnest in a president's second term.

> "I've heard it said that every president gets the White House that they deserve, and I do think that some of the way that [Trump] operates, the creative chaos . . . kind of freewheeling style, his penchant for putting two rival staff members in a room and letting them fight it out over an issue does breathe some of this competitive aspect."[16]
>
> —Former Trump aide Cliff Sims

Typical are the perils of serving as Trump's chief of staff. This person sets the president's schedule and manages the White House team. Reince Priebus, Trump's first choice, lasted barely six months in the job. Priebus reportedly was hemmed in by other staff members and endured mockery from the president. His replacement, retired general John Kelly, brought some order to the White House. But Kelly soon told friends that Trump was impossible to work with and the job was making him miserable. He resigned eighteen months into the job. Trump's next choice, Mick Mulvaney, formerly head of the budget office, promised to give the president more leeway to be himself. Some critics said that was the problem.

A Nontraditional Presidency

Experts believe one reason for the high turnover rate is the nature of Trump's campaign and presidency. They have been anything but traditional. He has sought from the first to disrupt things, to shake up a system he believes has grown stagnant and ineffective. Old Washington hands in the Republican Party who might have served in a more conventional administration instead have kept their distance. This has left Trump to assemble his cabinet and staff from those willing to risk their reputations in order to serve. Since Trump values loyalty over qualifications—in fact, over almost everything—an official is always one comment away from losing the boss's trust and his or her job.

Another way Trump departs from tradition is in the way he lets people go. Despite his volcanic temper, he declines to fire someone face-to-face. He dislikes personal confrontation, preferring instead to get the news out on Twitter—as with Secretary of State Rex Tillerson's firing—or pass the task to a staff member. "Although Trump once tried and failed to trademark the words, 'You're fired!'—his catchphrase from *The Apprentice*—it seems that he doesn't actually enjoy . . . replacing the loyalists that surround him," says political reporter Olivia Nuzzi. "Like so much with the president, it's shtick designed to make him look tough."[17]

Time and again Trump's combative nature has led him into controversy. He continually insults political foes and makes false

Changing Standards of News Reporting

Since taking office, Donald Trump has repeatedly called out the "fake news media" for its supposed bias against him. But many media outlets have indeed changed their approach to covering the news to deal with a president like no other in modern times. Certain newspapers and television news programs have abandoned strict objectivity in favor of coverage that treats the Trump administration as an adversary. The *New York Times* announced its new policy before Trump was elected. On August 8, 2016, the newspaper ran a front-page story by Jim Rutenberg headed "The Challenge Trump Poses to Objectivity." It began with the following question: "If you're a working journalist and you believe that Donald J. Trump is a demagogue playing to the nation's worst racist and nationalistic tendencies, that he cozies up to anti-American dictators and that he would be dangerous with control of the United States nuclear codes, how the heck are you supposed to cover him?"

From Rutenberg's article, it was obvious that the *New York Times* was changing its standards. It began calling Trump's dubious or inaccurate statements *lies*—a break from past practices. News stories about Trump often seemed to debate his points instead of simply reporting them. Meanwhile, the *Washington Post* adopted the tagline "Democracy Dies in Darkness" to highlight its mission to expose Trump's behavior, which some liken to that of authoritarian leaders. For Trump's opponents, these changes were perfectly acceptable. But they also led some to wonder whether Trump's complaints that he does not get a fair shake in the media are justified.

Quoted in Peter J. Boyer, "Donald Trump Changed *The New York Times*. Is It Forever?," *Esquire*, March 19, 2019. www.esquire.com.

statements on Twitter and in press conferences. His temperament and freewheeling style have helped make his administration chaotic and unpredictable. Turnover among his cabinet and staff has been remarkably high. Nonetheless, through all the turmoil, Trump's core supporters have stayed with him. They do not seem to mind that he is easily the most divisive president in decades.

CHAPTER TWO

Reversing Course in Foreign Policy

The White House meeting on May 13, 2019, seemed routine, with photo ops and a warm exchange between US president Donald Trump and Hungarian prime minister Viktor Orban. Trump held nothing back in his praise of Orban. He even compared his visitor to himself. "Viktor Orban has done a tremendous job in so many different ways," Trump said. "Highly respected. Respected all over Europe. Probably like me, a little bit controversial, but that's O.K. That's O.K. You've done a good job, and you've kept your country safe."[18]

However, Orban's visit was far from routine. He has been criticized both inside and outside of Hungary for right-wing assaults on democracy and the rule of law. His actions have made him an outcast among European leaders. He has railed against Muslim immigrants and vowed to preserve his country's Christian heritage. He has pursued closer ties with Vladimir Putin's Russia. Yet unlike presidents George W. Bush and Barack Obama, who refused to meet with Orban, Trump was willing to show support for the Hungarian strongman. It is one more example of how Trump has reversed course in American foreign policy.

> "Viktor Orban has done a tremendous job in so many different ways. Highly respected. Respected all over Europe. Probably like me, a little bit controversial, but that's O.K."[18]
>
> —Trump speaking at his meeting with Hungary's authoritarian leader Viktor Orban

A Strategy of "America First"

The roots of this reversal lie in nationalism. Trump is candid that his foreign policy is based on the idea of "America First." He rejects globalism—the idea that individual countries should be subordinate to global concerns and agreements. Instead he embraces a strong nationalism, promoting US interests above all others in everything from military alliances to economic pacts to immigration.

The word *nationalism* has a bad reputation from its links to fascist regimes in the 1930s and certain far-right governments of today. Yet Trump uses the term, along with the slogan America First, without apology. He believes that all nations should be honest about their self-interest and not pretend to be acting for the benefit of the world.

Trump and Prime Minister Viktor Orban of Hungary meet at the White House in 2019. Orban has been criticized inside and outside of Hungary for his assaults on democracy and the rule of law but Trump praised him for doing a "tremendous job."

Critics in the United States and Europe may cringe when Trump proclaims "America First," but his supporters regard the idea as common sense. According to Michael Anton, a former national security official in the Trump administration, "After all, what else is the purpose of any country's foreign policy except to put its own interests, the interests of its citizens, first?"[19]

Trump's critics insist the president has no guiding principle for his foreign policy. They note that he often acts on impulse or trusts his deal-making instincts to reach his goals. Nonetheless, he does have an overall strategy for foreign policy, an approach he calls "principled realism." In place of human rights and international cooperation, Trump focuses on keeping America strong and protecting its interests around the world. He rejects using military means to spread democracy, as the United States tried to do in the Iraq War. While not a complete isolationist—someone committed to avoiding military or economic ties to other countries—Trump believes the United States bears too large a burden when it comes to defending the West. "Right now, we are the policeman of the world and we're paying for it," he said following a December 2018 visit to American troops in Iraq. "And we can be the policeman of the world, but other countries have to help us."[20] He knows that most Americans are weary of Middle Eastern wars that seem to have no end. Far from the warmonger some painted him as in the campaign for the 2016 election, Trump has sought to reduce military engagement as much as possible.

> "After all, what else is the purpose of any country's foreign policy except to put its own interests, the interests of its citizens, first?"[19]
>
> —Michael Anton, former national security official in the Trump administration

Rethinking America's Alliances

Trump's approach has led him to question the value of alliances that go back decades. He sees NATO, which was formed after World War II to defend Europe against aggression by the Soviet Union, as an outdated concept. For Trump, Europe is more rival than partner in today's world. Moreover, he believes America's European allies are not paying their fair share to maintain NATO. Under the treaty, member states are required to spend at least 2 percent of their gross domestic product on defense. However, in 2017 only seven of the twenty-nine members met this spending requirement. That same year the United States accounted for more than 70 percent of defense spending among member nations. It poured more money into NATO than Germany, France, the United Kingdom, Italy, Spain, and Canada combined.

Trump's messages on NATO can be mixed, however. Despite his frequent criticism of America's NATO partners, Trump has also praised the unbreakable bond between the United States and its European allies. This praise was included in comments he made at a June 6, 2019, D-Day commemoration in France.

In March 2019 Trump also announced that going forward, allies must pay the full cost of hosting American troops, plus an extra fee of 50 percent for the privilege. US troops are stationed in allied countries mainly to deter aggression from hostile regimes, a policy that goes back to the Cold War with the Soviet Union. The Cost Plus 50 plan would force some allies to pay almost six times what they are now paying to house US troops. Trump's plan is aimed not only at longtime allies such as Germany and Japan but also smaller nations that have accepted American troops to deal with trouble spots. For example, in February 2019 South Korea agreed to pay nearly $1 billion each year to maintain American military personnel—but only after bitter talks that were almost derailed due to the new fees.

Trump's plan to hike the cost of hosting American soldiers has drawn fire from military experts and think tanks. They see it as one more way he is weakening longtime strategic alliances that have helped preserve peace in the world. Moreover, regarding American troops as soldiers for hire changes the tone of these agreements. "Previously, the United States treated host nations as partners who provided bases because of shared interests and oftentimes values, even if this was more of a façade than true," notes Stacie L. Pettyjohn, a senior political scientist at the Rand Corporation.

"The Cost Plus 50 approach instead appears to many to treat U.S. partners as client states that must pay for protection."[21]

Disdain for NATO and the European Union has led Trump to antagonize and even insult European leaders. He blasted German chancellor Angela Merkel for planning a new natural gas pipeline with Russia. He tweeted about the low approval ratings of French president Emmanuel Macron and reminded Macron that the United States had liberated France in World War II. He chastised British prime minister Theresa May for not following his advice on Brexit, the controversial British plan to exit the European Union. Europe's leaders have mostly tried to brush aside differences with Trump in public statements. But according to numerous reports in the European media, behind the scenes they and their advisers are appalled at his conduct.

Trump's repeated threats to withdraw from NATO and reduce America's commitments have alarmed Pentagon officials past and present. They know the value of these agreements and fear the consequences if the United States pulls out. Leaving NATO "would be one of the most damaging things that any president could do to U.S. interests," says Michéle A. Flournoy, an undersecretary of defense under Obama. "It would destroy 70-plus years of painstaking work across multiple administrations, Republican and Democratic, to create perhaps the most powerful and advantageous alliance in history. And it would be the wildest success that Vladimir Putin could dream of."[22]

Friendly Relations with Dictators

Not only has Trump been critical of longtime allies, he has also made friendly overtures to some of the world's worst dictators and authoritarian leaders. During a NATO summit in July 2018, he fist bumped Turkey's autocrat Recep Tayyip Erdogan and praised him for doing things the right way. In October 2018, after political journalist Jamal Khashoggi was brutally murdered by agents of Saudi Arabia inside the Saudi consulate in Turkey, Trump rushed to defend Saudi ruler Mohammed bin Salman. Investigators later

Trump and Israel

Trump's critics have accused him of all sorts of bigotry, including anti-Semitism. Yet Trump's daughter and son-in-law and their three children are Orthodox Jews. Moreover, Trump has shown consistent support for Israel and its prime minister, Benjamin Netanyahu. Trump took office determined to repair relations with Israel, following eight years of the Obama administration in which the US-Israeli alliance was strained to the breaking point. Trump wasted little time in demonstrating the change. On December 6, 2017, he recognized Jerusalem as the capital of Israel and moved the American embassy to Jerusalem from Tel Aviv. The move, which Trump insisted was long overdue, angered Palestinians who claim East Jerusalem as capital of their planned independent state. Trump's announcement drew quick condemnation from many world leaders. There were also predictions of violence, but the move proceeded without disruption.

There have been other displays of solidarity. Trump backed Israeli control of a disputed area on the Syrian border called the Golan Heights. His decision to pull out of the multinational Iran nuclear energy deal delighted Israelis who feared it actually increased the likelihood of an Iranian nuclear weapon. Nevertheless, most American Jews strongly disapprove of Trump, and his policies toward Israel have not changed their minds. According to a Pew Research Center analysis, 79 percent of American Jews voted for Democrats in the midterm elections. Trump is actually more popular among Israelis than American Jews. A 2019 poll conducted by the Pew Research Center shows that 82 percent of Israeli Jews have confidence in his leadership.

---

found that Salman likely had ordered the killing. At a political fund raiser in Florida in March 2018, Trump jokingly approved of how Chinese president Xi Jinping had cemented his place as dictator. "He's now president for life. President for life. No, he's great," Trump said. "And look, he was able to do that. I think it's great. Maybe we'll have to give that a shot some day."[23] To the media, it was part of a curious pattern of going easy on autocrats.

Chief among these is Vladimir Putin, a former Soviet intelligence official who has ruled Russia since 1999. The Russian president was one of the first world leaders to congratulate Trump on his victory in the 2016 election. At a 2017 economic meeting in Vietnam, Trump chatted with Putin and reported later that Putin had assured him Russia had not meddled in the American presidential election.

In July 2018 the two leaders met in Helsinki, Finland, for their first official summit. Afterward, they held a joint press conference in which Trump refused to criticize Putin and even questioned US intelligence findings that Russia had indeed interfered in the election. Trump's remarks set off a firestorm in the United States. John Brennan, CIA director under Obama, considered them treasonous and grounds for impeachment. Republican senator Jeff Flake admitted, "I never thought I would see the day when our American

Trump and Russian president Vladimir Putin give a joint news conference in Helsinki, Finland, in 2018. Trump refused to criticize or even question Russia's interference in the 2016 presidential election.

President would stand on the stage with the Russian President and place blame on the United States for Russian aggression. This is shameful."[24] Trump's own advisers admitted they were shocked by the press conference.

In November 2018 Trump did criticize Russian aggression in Ukraine, and he canceled a personal meeting with Putin at the G20 conference in Buenos Aires, Argentina. He also has sold defensive weapons to Ukraine, slapped Russia with tough sanctions, and withdrawn from a missile treaty he claims Putin was no longer honoring. In Trump's view, it is best to maintain somewhat friendly relations with an authoritarian leader like Putin while also holding no illusions about his intent. Nonetheless, critics have expressed outrage at Trump's refusal to denounce a person they see as a dangerous enemy.

> "I never thought I would see the day when our American President would stand on the stage with the Russian President and place blame on the United States for Russian aggression. This is shameful."[24]
>
> —Republican senator Jeff Flake

Negotiating with North Korea

Trump has reversed course with another American foe, North Korea's Kim Jong Un. Past US presidents had declined to engage with Kim personally, preferring to deal through representatives. Foreign policy experts felt a face-to-face meeting with the unpredictable North Korean dictator would only give him added prestige on the world stage. However, Trump took a more personal approach from the start.

In September 2017 North Korea tested nuclear weapons for the sixth time. Kim also claimed his country had developed nuclear missiles that could reach the US mainland with the push of a button. On January 2, 2018, Trump responded to Kim's boast with his own threat via Twitter: "North Korean Leader Kim Jong Un just stated that the 'Nuclear Button is on his desk at all times.' Will someone from his depleted and food starved regime please inform him that I too have a Nuclear Button, but it is a much big-

> "Will someone from his depleted and food starved regime please inform him that I too have a Nuclear Button, but it is a much bigger & more powerful one than his, and my Button works!"[25]
>
> —Trump responding on Twitter to North Korean leader Kim Jong Un

ger & more powerful one than his, and my Button works!"[25] Trump also swore to rain down fire and fury on North Korea should it attack the United States.

Experts mocked Trump's schoolyard taunts—especially with regard to nuclear missiles—and feared he might be placing US ally South Korea in danger. But as is so often the case with Trump, his swaggering threats were merely an opening gambit. He surprised the world by agreeing to meet with Kim in the first-ever summit between the two nations. On June 12, 2018, the two leaders met in Singapore, signing a joint declaration to pursue peace and eliminate nuclear weapons on the Korean Peninsula. Trump joked afterward that he and Kim "fell in love."[26]

This meeting and a second summit in February 2019 produced no binding deals but did seem to reduce tensions. Kim had held off from further nuclear tests for more than seventeen months, but he resumed testing tactical weapons in May 2019. "Kim Jong Un knows Trump's weakness," says Chun Yung-woo, former national security adviser in South Korea. "Trump claims that it is his achievement that North Korea stopped testing missiles and nuclear weapons. Showing Kim can resume the tests is the scariest card Kim can play."[27]

Rejecting the Iran Nuclear Pact

One of Trump's most controversial moves has been to exit the 2015 Iran nuclear agreement, the centerpiece of Obama's foreign policy. Under the pact, Iran agreed to certain restrictions on its nuclear program, designed to keep the Iranians from secretly developing nuclear weapons with enriched uranium. In return Iran received relief from harsh economic sanctions that had been crippling its oil-based economy. Parties to the agreement included Iran, the United States, the United Kingdom, France, China, Rus-

Crisis in Venezuela

One potential crisis Trump faces lies in his own hemisphere. Venezuela, once the richest nation in Latin America with vast amounts of oil wealth, now stands on the brink of economic collapse. The socialist policies of President Hugo Chávez and his successor, Nicolás Maduro, have plunged the nation into ruin. Despair about the situation, including skyrocketing inflation and shortages of basic goods, led the people to take to the streets in huge protests. On January 23, 2019, Trump officially recognized the leader of the opposition, Juan Guaidó, as the legitimate president of Venezuela. As Trump noted, "The people of Venezuela have courageously spoken out against Maduro and his regime and demanded freedom and the rule of law." Following Trump's announcement, a number of countries joined with the United States in accepting Guaidó and urging Maduro to relinquish power.

However, Maduro has refused to go. As of now, he retains the support of most of the Venezuelan military along with troops from Cuba and Russia. In response, the Trump administration has placed sanctions on the Maduro regime, cutting it off from needed financing. As tensions rise in the region, Trump and his advisers hope Venezuelan military officers will defect to the people's side and allow for peaceful democratic change. However, as US Secretary of State Mike Pompeo declared, "Military action is possible. If that's what's required, that's what the United States will do." Venezuela may turn out to be the unlikely site of Trump's first military crisis.

Quoted in Kaitlan Collins and Kevin Liptak, "Trump Urges Caution as Bolton and Pompeo Tease a Military Intervention in Venezuela," CNN, May 3, 2019. www.cnn.com.

---

sia, and Germany.

In May 2018 Trump announced the United States' withdrawal from the pact. By doing so, he was honoring one of his early campaign promises. He had long criticized the agreement as one-sided in Iran's favor, with too many loopholes that enabled the Iranians to cheat. In place of the deal, Trump reimposed sanctions and made them considerably tougher. The goal was to drive Iranian oil exports down to almost zero. In making the move, Trump was drawing on his recent success in pressuring Kim and North Korea to the bargaining table. Trump was willing to renegotiate a better deal in order to put the clamps on Iran's ability to manufacture a nuclear weapon. Backing the president's strategy was a new, more hawkish foreign policy team, which included Secretary of State Mike Pompeo and National Security Adviser John Bolton.

Trump's announcement drew criticism at home and abroad. In a rare public rebuke, Obama declared that scrapping the deal would leave the United States with a bad choice between a nuclear Iran and war in the Middle East. European leaders protested as well, begging Trump to reconsider. Iran's mullahs, the religious leaders in control of the nation, declared they would continue to abide by the deal, as did the other nations that had signed the agreement. Trump officials and Republican leaders maintained that Iran was a rogue regime, cracking down on protesters at home and spreading violence through terrorist militias in Lebanon, Syria, Iraq, and Yemen. Trump's State Department designated Iran's Islamic Revolutionary Guard Corps (basically the Iranian military) as a foreign terrorist group.

In May 2019 the Trump administration blamed Iran for sabotage attacks on oil tankers near the Strait of Hormuz in the Persian Gulf. The following month saw Iran shoot down a $110 million US drone aircraft over the strait. US planes were ready to launch a military strike against Iran in retaliation, but Trump called off the strike at the last moment due to concerns about Iranian casualties. Afterward Trump stressed that he did not want war with Iran. Yet he warned the mullahs not to engage in any further attacks and proceeded to ratchet up economic sanctions on the Iranian regime. He also revealed the US had targeted Iran's military computer systems with a sophisticated cyberattack. Meanwhile, Trump's Democratic opponents in Congress feared that the president, despite his words to the contrary, was leading the United States into war with Iran. "Look at what they've done: Walked away from the agreement we had with allies, unlikely allies, all around the world to stop the development of nuclear weapons

An oil tanker burns in the Gulf of Oman, near the strategic Strait of Hormuz, in June 2019. The Trump administration accused Iran of attacking two vessels. These events contributed to heightened tensions between Iran and the United States.

in Iran," says Democratic senator Dick Durbin. "I can tell you this senator and many like me are going to resist any effort to engage the United States in another war in the Middle East."[28]

Trump has reversed the course of American foreign policy in many areas. With his slogan of America First, he has questioned the usefulness of longtime alliances and urged allies to pay more for their own defense. Trump also has pursued friendly relations with authoritarian leaders and dictators. His erratic diplomacy features blustering threats on the one hand and willingness to negotiate on the other. His habit of making impulsive decisions continues to create uncertainty in America's foreign relations.

CHAPTER THREE

Illegal Immigration and Building the Wall

On April 5, 2019, Trump met with law enforcement and immigration officials in the border town of Calexico, California. It was another in a series of visits to the US-Mexico border to highlight what Trump called "a colossal surge"[29] of illegal immigrants into the United States. According to US Customs and Border Protection numbers, agents had apprehended more than one hundred thousand illegal crossers in March, a twelve-year high. The El Centro sector in Southern California had seen an almost 400 percent increase in families arriving from Mexico and Central America. In recent days Trump had threatened to shut down the border if Mexico refused to halt the migrant flood and if Congress failed to fix loopholes in immigration laws. Besides the roundtable discussion with officials, Trump also inspected a 2-mile (3.2 km) stretch of recently rebuilt 30-foot-high (9.1 m) fencing designed to thwart illegal crossings. During his visit, he delivered a pointed message to prospective immigrants from the south: "Whether it's asylum, whether it's anything you want, it's illegal immigration, can't take you anymore. Our country is full, our area is full, the sector is full, can't take you anymore. I'm sorry, can't happen, so turn around—that's the way it is."[30]

Frustration and Anger

One reason for Trump's election was the way he tapped into widespread frustration about controlling the border with Mexico. His vows to stop illegal immigration came as a welcome change to voters who had lost patience with years of government inaction and lack of seriousness about people coming across the border illegally. At campaign rallies, Trump's promise to build a wall and make Mexico pay for it drew some of the largest roars of approval. Whether the proposed barrier is a wall, a fence, a series of concrete slabs or steel slats, a line of electronic sensors, or some other arrangement, Trump's supporters want the southern border fortified against illegal entry. They are bitterly opposed to what they see as a Democratic push for open borders. At bottom they agree with the president's tweet of June 19, 2018: "If you don't have Borders, you don't have a Country!"[31]

> "If you don't have Borders, you don't have a Country!"[31]
>
> —Trump's June 19, 2018, tweet on border control

Trump's supporters also want tougher enforcement measures, including more border patrol agents and increased surveillance. They are wary of compromises that would allow undocumented immigrants who are already here to become citizens. Even when federal courts block Trump's efforts to police the border, his supporters stay with him. Some compare the issue to how sensible homeowners deal with neighbors. "It's the same that you would do in your house," says Maria Guadalupe Dempsey, a Trump Republican who lives in the West Texas county of Hudspeth, only a footbridge away from Valle de Juárez in Mexico. "You build a fence, you put a gate up and you open and close it as you wish. You invite people in. You don't want people who are not invited to come into the country."[32]

Attack on American Values

Trump's opponents reject his views about immigration and border security. To them, his stance is an attack on core American values such as tolerance and charity. They stress that the United States is almost entirely a nation of immigrants, with a long tradition of welcoming those who are seeking a better life.

Many on the left support so-called sanctuary cities, whose laws help prevent undocumented immigrants from being arrested or deported by federal agents. They blame Trump's immigration policies for what they consider a calamity on the southern border.

Overall, Trump's opponents often link his calls for border security to racial bias and white supporters' fears about the changing racial profile of America. Many have noted Trump's attempts to paint Hispanic immigrants as criminals. "When Mexico sends its people, they're not sending their best," he told the crowd at his 2015 presidential announcement speech at Trump Tower in New York City. "They're sending people that have lots of problems, and they're bringing those problems with [them]. They're bringing drugs. They're bringing crime. They're rapists. And some, I assume, are good people."[33]

Workers in Calexico, California, repair razor wire atop the fence that separates the United States from Mexico. Trump has vowed to build a wall to stop illegal entries, a project his supporters see as critical to the nation's future.

Opponents insist such remarks only spread fear and distrust. According to Douglas Rivlin, communications director of America's Voice, an immigrant-advocacy group, "If you think immigrants are welcome in our country, you are not welcome in the Republican Party—that seems to be the bottom line."[34]

> "If you think immigrants are welcome in our country, you are not welcome in the Republican Party—that seems to be the bottom line."[34]
>
> —Douglas Rivlin, communications director of America's Voice, an immigrant-advocacy group

Americans generally oppose Trump's immigration policies, including the border wall proposal. In a January 2019 Quinnipiac poll, a majority said that building a border wall is not a good use of taxpayer dollars, is not necessary for security, and goes against American values. Yet according to a January 2019 ABC News/*Washington Post* poll, a majority also believes the government is not doing enough to keep people from entering the country illegally. And two-thirds of Americans agree the southern border is not secure. These results ensure that immigration will remain a crucial—and bitterly divisive—issue for the Trump administration.

Zero-Tolerance Policy

Trump's policy for dealing with illegal immigration is defined by two words: *zero tolerance*. Then-attorney general Jeff Sessions announced the administration's new policy in April 2018 before a gathering of sheriffs from US counties that border Mexico. The federal government aimed to apprehend and prosecute anyone who crossed the border illegally, with no exceptions. This meant that immigrants who crossed at places other than designated ports of entry, including those seeking legal asylum, would be detained. Those found to be already in the country illegally were also subject to arrest. Border patrol officers immediately began rounding up offenders.

However, the Trump administration failed to lay the groundwork for such a radical plan. The policy caught many government agencies by surprise. These included the US Department of

Homeland Security (DHS), which arrests and holds undocumented immigrants, and the US Department of Health and Human Services, which cares for migrant children whose parents are arrested. There was almost no preparation for the new procedures. As a result, as many as three thousand children were separated from their families after being apprehended at the border. This action was due to statutes that forbid the keeping of children in jail with their parents. Thus, while immigrant parents awaited their day in court, their children were shuttled off to other facilities, sometimes hundreds of miles away.

Whether Trump's policy was intended to pressure Democrats to support border controls or to warn off potential immigrants, it quickly backfired. Outrage at the idea of separating families, regardless of their legal status, led to weeks of national protests. As the number of detainees grew, some children were moved into makeshift fenced enclosures. Pundits on both the left and right expressed disbelief at the sight of children held in cages in America. (Photos posted on social media showed that immigrant children had also been confined in fenced areas on military bases during the Obama administration.) The *New York Post*'s editorial page, typically supportive of Trump, admitted, "It's not just that this looks terrible in the eyes of the world. It *is* terrible."[35] First Lady Melania Trump remarked, "We need to be a country that follows all laws, but also one that governs with heart."[36]

Problems with Catch and Release

Trump's zero-tolerance policy soon drew rebukes from federal judges. One court ruled that the separation of families at the border must end at once. Trump complied by issuing a new executive order that kept families together but sought to detain them indefinitely while legal proceedings went forward. However, US district judge Dolly Gee demanded that the administration follow prior rulings that forbade the holding of migrant children longer than twenty days. Trump officials claimed that they needed more time to reunite children with their families, but the judge held firm.

Trump has protested that the court's ruling would block his attempts to control the border as he was elected to do. If a family of undocumented immigrants must stay together, and if the children can only be held for twenty days, then the entire family has to be released while they await a court hearing. However, as Trump contends, many such families melt into the border towns and never show up in court. For Trump, this practice, which he mockingly calls "catch and release," undermines his immigration policies. George W. Bush and Barack Obama also faced this problem in policing illegal border crossings. Trump has blamed the Obama administration for creating a loophole in immigration law by releasing whole families with no supervision. In any case, Trump supporters claim that Central American families have come to see catch and release as their ticket to illegal entry into the United States.

Thousands of people march in 2018 in Washington, DC, to protest the Trump administration's zero-tolerance policy for illegal immigration. Under this policy, children were forcibly separated from their parents.

The Muslim Ban

Another Trump controversy related to foreigners coming to the United States is the so-called Muslim ban. One week after his inauguration in January 2017, the president signed an executive order that barred people from seven Middle Eastern and African nations from entering the United States for at least ninety days. The seven nations in the original ban—Iran, Iraq, Libya, Somalia, Sudan, Syria, and Yemen—all were Muslim majority. The purpose of the ban, Trump said, was to stop potential terrorists from entering the United States until travelers could be screened more effectively. As Trump administration officials noted, all seven countries harbored terrorist groups such as al Qaeda, the Islamic State, and al Shabaab.

Trump's order set off massive protests nationwide. Opponents accused Trump of discriminating against Muslims. Immigration lawyers filed suit to halt Trump's action. District judges in several states, including New York, Massachusetts, and Hawaii, blocked the order temporarily. Critics of the policy pointed out that the perpetrators of the 9/11 attacks all came from Saudi Arabia, yet that country was not included in the ban. The intense reaction seemed to catch the White House off guard. After only a few days in office, Trump had set off a firestorm.

In June 2018 the Supreme Court allowed a watered-down version of Trump's travel ban to remain in place. Chief Justice John Roberts noted that the policy "covers just 8% of the world's Muslim population and is limited to countries that were previously designated by Congress or prior administrations as posing national security risks."

Quoted in Adam Serwer, "The Supreme Court's Green Light to Discriminate," *Atlantic*, June 26, 2018. www.theatlantic.com.

The Dreamers Dilemma

Another immigration question for Trump is what to do with the so-called Dreamers. These are young people whose parents brought them across the border illegally and who have lived in the United States almost all their lives. Their current status is in limbo. Some Americans want them immediately deported, while others believe they deserve full citizenship. Most people favor a solution somewhere in between.

In 2012 Obama created a program called Deferred Action for Childhood Arrivals (DACA) to protect these young adults from deportation. DACA does not provide a path to citizenship or confer official legal status. However, those who receive DACA status can legally apply for work permits and driver's licenses. In September 2017 Attorney General Jeff Sessions announced that the Trump administration was ending the program. At the same time Trump urged Congress to replace DACA with a bill to protect the Dreamers before they would become eligible for deportation in March 2018. At this time they numbered more than seven hundred thousand, with 80 percent originally from Mexico. Yet in the following months, Trump seemed to change his mind again. He rejected several compromise bills that would have addressed the problem. Meanwhile, federal judges in California, New York, and Washington, DC, made rulings that allowed people who had filed for DACA status to renew. The Trump administration has urged the Supreme Court to hear its case about ending the DACA program.

In bargaining on the DACA issue, Trump has steered between extremes. Many Democrats will not be satisfied until Dreamers are granted a pathway to citizenship. Trump's conservative supporters warn that amnesty for Dreamers—allowing them to stay and become citizens—will encourage more illegal immigrants to cross the border and bring their young children.

In December 2018 bitter disagreement in Congress over funding to build Trump's wall led to a government shutdown. Thirty days into the shutdown, Trump offered to extend protections for Dreamers for three years in exchange for $5.7 billion in border wall funds. However, Democrats refused to budge on funding the wall. As for the Dreamers, they remained in limbo. "It's an insult when [Trump's] offering something we already had and he took away," says Juan Prieto, a DACA recipient and spokesperson for the California Immigrant Youth Justice Alliance. "We don't want our lives and the promise of temporary fixes to be used for permanent damage," he adds, referring to the border wall. "That's what's happening here."[37]

Caravans and Crisis

No sooner had Trump agreed to end the government shutdown than another crisis loomed at the southern border. Caravans of migrants from all over Central America were making their way to the border. The caravans included long lines of individuals and families trekking on foot across hundreds of miles of rugged terrain. Some of the travelers hoped to get asylum in the United

In 2019 a caravan consisting of hundreds of Central American migrants slowly makes its way through Mexico toward the United States. Many of the migrants, including a large number of families, were seeking asylum in the United States.

States after escaping from violent drug gangs or government thugs in their own countries. They bore scars from machete slashes and bullet wounds. Others simply wanted to reach the United States and somehow gain entry and obtain a better paying job. The size of the caravans swelled to include hundreds and even thousands of travelers.

Some questioned the timing of this enormous migration and wondered who was funding the migrants. Activist groups like Pueblo sin Fronteras (City without Borders) were known to coach Central American migrants on how to flee their countries and apply for asylum in the United States. However, the caravans seemed to be loosely organized. The migrants walked for days, with little food and uncertain shelter at night. As journalist Sophia Lee noted, "Border Patrol agents report that when they apprehend these people at the border, the kids look malnourished and the adults look haggard, as though they've survived famine and war. Many need immediate medical attention."[38]

In response to the caravans, Trump declared a national emergency at the southern border. He charged that only a small percentage of the migrants had legitimate asylum claims. The president also announced that he was slashing aid to the Central American countries of El Salvador, Guatemala, and Honduras for their failure to slow the migration. Democrats in Congress blasted the move as likely to make the situation worse and lead to more caravans. Meanwhile, US Customs and Border Protection agents were swamped with new arrivals. More than 100,000 migrants were apprehended in March 2019 and in May nearly 145,000, numbers not seen for twelve years. Mark Morgan, who served as border patrol chief under Obama, told a Senate committee the situation was out of control. "We're experiencing a crisis at the southern border

> "Border Patrol agents report that when they apprehend these people at the border, the kids look malnourished and the adults look haggard, as though they've survived famine and war. Many need immediate medical attention."[38]
>
> —Journalist Sophia Lee on migrant caravans that travel to the US border

Making Mexico Pay for the Wall

At Trump's political rallies, his promise to build a border wall and make Mexico pay for it drew hearty cheers. But the president has found this promise difficult to keep. Both Mexican presidents during Trump's term, Enrique Peña Nieto and his successor, Andrés Manuel López Obrador, repeatedly have said their country has no intention of paying for a wall. In response Trump has backtracked and claimed he never said Mexico would pay directly as in writing a check; instead he would force them to fund the wall in indirect ways, with tariffs on goods and other economic penalties. At one point he even planned to seize money for the wall from the billions that Mexican nationals in the United States wire home to their families in Mexico each year. The plan would also have raised fees on border crossing cards and worker visas for Mexicans.

In the end this scheme was rejected as impractical and unlikely to pass legal muster. Nonetheless, Trump continues to seek ways to punish Mexico for what he sees as its share in the border crisis. On May 29, 2019, Trump tweeted his intention to slap a 5 percent tariff on all Mexican goods coming into the United States. To forestall the new tariff, Mexico agreed to step up its efforts to control the flow of migrants through its territory. Yet Mexican officials refused to overreact to Trump's threats. "It is no secret that Trump is very active in his use of Twitter," says trade negotiator Jesus Seade, "and he launches many tweets that are later changed."

Quoted in Katherine Faulders et al., "Trump Defends 5% Tariff Threat as Mexico's President Calls It a 'Provocation' and GOP Senator Slams It as a Misuse of Authority," ABC News, May 31, 2019. www.abcnews.go.com.

at a magnitude never seen in modern times, it's unprecedented," said Morgan. "We're letting in tens of thousands of people into this country every day who we know virtually nothing about."[39]

Overhaul of the Immigration Team

The border crisis also led to an overhaul of Trump's immigration team. In April 2019 Kirstjen Nielsen, secretary of the DHS, resigned abruptly. Trump announced he wanted a more aggressive direction for the DHS, US Immigration and Customs Enforcement, and other agencies that deal with immigration and border issues. He promised to get a barrier of some kind built even if he had to issue an executive order for the purpose. Critics warned that compassion as well as toughness would be needed to ease the humanitarian crisis at the border.

Trump's immigration policy has been a constant source of controversy since he took office. His zero-tolerance approach to illegal immigration has tapped into the anger and frustration of voters who favor border controls. His crusade to build a wall on the southern border has pleased his supporters and exasperated his detractors. Endless negotiations with Congress over possible fixes to immigration policy have gone nowhere and have even led to a government shutdown. Issues with Dreamers and caravans of migrants seeking asylum have only added to the confusion. As the situation on the border grows more chaotic, the Trump administration is certain to face more pressure to act.

> "We're experiencing a crisis at the southern border at a magnitude never seen in modern times, it's unprecedented. We're letting in tens of thousands of people into this country every day who we know virtually nothing about."[39]
>
> —Mark Morgan, border patrol chief under President Barack Obama

CHAPTER FOUR

Tax Cuts and Tariffs for the Economy

To boost the American economy, Trump has tried to ensure that other nations compete fairly in the open marketplace. In pursuit of this goal, Trump has punished foreign companies he sees as the worst offenders with regard to unfair business practices. On May 15, 2019, Trump issued an executive order prohibiting American companies from selling products and equipment to certain foreign tech firms. These included Huawei, a huge Chinese technology company that is the world's second-largest smartphone supplier. The Trump administration has repeatedly accused Huawei of stealing American technology, including patented software and parts for its smartphones. China also is suspected of using Huawei devices to spy on America and its allies. The move was aimed at showing that Trump's patience with Chinese double-dealing was at an end. It was typical of his combative approach to trade and the economy.

Bold Steps, Impulsive Actions

News of the ban sent tech stocks tumbling in the United States. Experts warned that Trump's move could affect complicated global supply chains. American technology companies like Apple, Google, and Qualcomm were looking at huge, and very costly, disruptions. In addition, there was the threat of Chinese retaliation. Not for the first time, the Trump administration had to backtrack on a sudden policy change. Days after the original order, the US Department of Commerce announced a ninety-day temporary license allowing Huawei to buy equipment and software updates for its smartphone users. Tech executives cheered the pullback, but they also were uneasy at Trump's impulsive order. "The more that we continually conflate economic warfare with national security interests, then we start to look at everything as national security," says Evanna Hu, CEO of Omelas, a US security software firm based in Washington, DC. "When you have a hammer, everything looks like a nail."[40]

As with the Huawei ban, Trump's America First philosophy guides his approach to the economy. It has led him to take bold steps, such as slashing corporate tax rates, to help American businesses be more competitive worldwide. It also has spurred him to rethink America's trade deals and sometimes scrap them in favor of new agreements. He prides himself on being a champion deal maker. However, his aggressive use of tariffs—fees for goods imported into the United States to punish trading partners—is often impulsive and results in retaliatory measures that hurt American manufacturers and farmers.

A Strong Economy

Forecasts of economic disaster and recession following Trump's surprising election victory have proved to be mistaken. In general, the US economy has performed well under Trump. It has forged ahead even while global output has slowed. For example, in 2018 US gross domestic product (GDP) grew at a rate of 2.9 percent. Consumer spending has been strong, and unemployment is at its lowest level in decades. Inflation remains modest, and wages are inching upward. Trump's focus on American workers and products has encouraged some US manufacturers and defense contractors to use American products, raw materials, and labor, which has helped boost jobs and wages for blue-collar workers. He has promoted this success in characteristic fashion on Twitter: "The economy is soooo good, perhaps the best in our country's history (remember, it's the economy stupid!)."[41]

Economists disagree on how much credit Trump deserves for the healthy economy. Liberal economists stress that when Trump took office, the economy had been growing steadily since recovering from the Great Recession of 2008. This contradicts his claims that he inherited an economic mess from Obama. However, conservative economists point out that growth had

The Chinese technology company Huawei was at the center of a trade dispute between the United States and China in 2019. The Trump administration has accused Huawei, the world's second-largest smartphone supplier, of stealing American technology.

slowed to 1.6 percent in Obama's final year in office. They also contend that Obama's policies actually held back the recovery, which should have been more robust after such a deep recession. According to economists Stephen Moore and Arthur Laffer, "Mr. Obama might be justified in taking credit for today's economy if his successor had adopted and carried on his policies. Instead, Mr. Trump has reversed nearly every Obama rule, edict and law that he can legally overturn. . . . As a result, the economy [has popped] like a cork pulled from a shaken champagne bottle."[42]

> "Mr. Trump has reversed nearly every Obama rule, edict and law that he can legally overturn. . . . As a result, the economy [has popped] like a cork pulled from a shaken champagne bottle."[42]
>
> —Economists Stephen Moore and Arthur Laffer

Polls show that the economy is Trump's best issue with American voters. In a January 2019 CNN poll, 56 percent of Americans said they approve of the job he is doing on the economy, one of his highest poll numbers since taking office. At the same time, 54 percent have a negative opinion of Trump overall.

A Program of Tax Relief

A key part of Trump's economic plan is tax relief, or lower tax rates. On the campaign trail in 2016, Trump pointed out that the US corporate tax rate was one of the highest in the world—nearly 39 percent when federal and state taxes were combined. He claimed that lower rates were necessary to help American companies compete in the global marketplace. This in turn would enable them to provide more jobs. In addition, Trump promised to lower taxes for working families in America.

The Republican-controlled Senate passed Trump's tax reform bill on December 20, 2017. Corporate tax rates were sliced to about 24 percent (federal plus state average), while individual rates also fell. Polls at the time showed that more than half of Americans opposed the plan. Democrats complained that the bill eased the tax burden on large businesses and high earners while doing little to help the middle class. New Jersey senator Cory Booker said the plan would make inequality in America worse, not better. Booker called the bill "irresponsible, reckless, unjust, and just plain cruel."[43] And Vermont senator Bernie Sanders fumed, "We are witnessing highway robbery in broad daylight and a looting of the Federal Treasury."[44]

Nonetheless, Trump's tax plan mostly had the desired effect. It kick-started economic activity and boosted GDP. Individual income tax collections soared, reaching an all-time high of $1.7 trillion for fiscal year 2018. Corporations such as Apple and Microsoft finally paid billions in taxes on profits that had been parked overseas for years. The plan also helped create jobs and led to the lowest unemployment rate in a generation. Job creation, one of Trump's main themes, benefited all groups. Black unemployment dropped to 5.9 percent, the lowest level since the government began tracking it in 1972. Hispanic unemployment was also down.

The tax plan was not without drawbacks. Due to lower rates, corporate tax collections fell by nearly one-third. As a result, federal tax revenues overall rose by only 0.5 percent. With increased government spending, the budget deficit (the negative balance between revenues and spending) grew by $113 billion and seemed certain to continue its rise. Trump's opponents howled that his plan was a giveaway to the rich, but supporters focused on the benefits. As the *Investor's Business Daily* wrote, "So, the question is: Would it have been better to have kept taxes high, and sacrificed economic, job and wage gains we've been enjoying, so that the government could have collected a little bit more in taxes?"[45]

> "So, the question is: Would it have been better to have kept taxes high, and sacrificed economic, job and wage gains we've been enjoying, so that the government could have collected a little bit more in taxes?"[45]
>
> —*Investor's Business Daily*

Job seekers fill out applications at a job fair. The 2017 tax reform bill lowered tax rates for many US companies. Trump and congressional Republicans said this would make those companies more competitive and thus more likely to create new jobs.

Cutting Regulations

Alongside tax reform, Trump has focused on easing government regulations on business and investment. He believes American companies need relief from the blizzard of rules that federal agencies in Washington, DC, issue each year. Freed from all that red tape, businesses could concentrate on expanding and providing jobs. To this end, Trump addressed the regulations problem in his second week in office. He signed an executive order that said any new regulation must be offset by getting rid of two prior ones. In its first year, Trump's new policy delayed or canceled almost sixteen hundred planned regulations. And the two-for-one goal actually ended up closer to four-for-one in the ratio of major regulations canceled to new ones.

Many small business owners consider the new policy a major improvement. They believe it helps them divert less time and money to filling out forms and checking for compliance. It also eases concerns about having to fight some new government rule.

Tax Relief for the Middle Class

Trump promoted his Tax Cuts and Jobs Act as benefiting not only big business but also middle-class taxpayers. Under the plan, individual taxpayers got lower rates and a doubled standard deduction (the portion of personal income shielded from tax). Trump supporters claim the tax bill has been an unqualified success for the middle class. They point to higher wages, increased take-home pay, more jobs, added employee benefits, and new feelings of optimism about job security. With the economy growing more robustly, wages have jumped 3.2 percent, and job openings reached a new high of 7.3 million in January 2019. Trump, say his supporters, deserves credit for a resurgence of the middle class in America.

Trump's opponents, however, paint a picture that is much more downbeat. They insist most middle-class taxpayers barely noticed the slight change in their rates. The increased personal deduction served mainly to take the place of mortgage deductions and may have hurt the housing industry. Changes in withholding rules for paychecks can also result in a smaller tax refund for individuals, leading many middle-class taxpayers to feel like their taxes were raised, not lowered. "Ask people how much they paid in taxes, nobody knows. Ask them how much they got in their refund, people know," says Howard Gleckman, a senior fellow at the Tax Policy Center. Trump's opponents point to the midterm elections—in which Democrats retook control of the House of Representatives—as proof of public dissatisfaction with Trump's economic and other policies.

Quoted in Eric Levitz, "Trump Tax Cuts Are (Probably) About to Become a Political Disaster," *New York*, February 8, 2019. www.nymag.com.

Experts say deregulation may not boost profits directly, but it certainly can help. "The notion that deregulation unleashes growth is virtually impossible to find in the data," says Jared Bernstein, a senior fellow at the Center on Budget and Policy Priorities. "What does matter is this idea that confidence matters. If [business owners'] expectations about the future are positive, then it does make a difference."[46]

Critics of Trump's deregulation efforts say they endanger the environment, personal privacy, and consumer protection. For example, getting rid of rules about dumping mining waste in streams may benefit the coal industry, but it can also pollute waterways and endanger public health. Likewise, easing restrictions on Internet companies that sell customers' browser histories can lead to loss of privacy. Trump foes fear his antiregulation crusade could threaten everything from workplace safety to protections for overtime pay. "These deregulatory efforts are not seeking to create jobs," says Sam Berger, senior adviser at the Center for American Progress. "They are not aimed at improving the lives of middle-class Americans or spurring economic growth. Rather, they seek to eliminate important safeguards in order to encourage an economy in which it's easier for big businesses to make money by cheating their clients and stealing from their workers."[47]

> "[Trump's deregulatory efforts] seek to eliminate important safeguards in order to encourage an economy in which it's easier for big businesses to make money by cheating their clients and stealing from their workers."[47]
>
> —Sam Berger, senior adviser at the Center for American Progress

Remaking Trade Agreements

Trump's America First philosophy also guides his approach to trade agreements. He seeks to renegotiate deals in order to secure more favorable terms for the United States. His brash and freewheeling approach to talks has led to friction with America's longtime trading partners. In general Trump's view is that they need the United States more than the United States needs them.

One of his most controversial moves was pulling out of the Trans-Pacific Partnership (TPP), a twelve-nation trade deal negotiated by the Obama administration. Trump had blasted the agreement repeatedly on the campaign trail. He claimed it was bad for American workers and manufacturers and promised to pull the plug once in office. Congress had yet to ratify the TPP when Trump scrapped it in January 2017, and the outlook for the deal was already bleak. Most Democrats opposed it, and many Republicans found themselves caught between their support for the president and their own free-trade beliefs.

Still, experts on globalization argued that the agreement was America's best opportunity to offset China's increasing influence on global trade. With the United States pulling out, other nations in the TPP set about creating a valuable network of mutual deals. Meanwhile, American companies had to pay higher tariffs in order to get their products into TPP member nations such as Japan, Australia, and New Zealand. "That means that Welch's grape juice, Tyson's pork and California almonds will remain subject to tariffs in Japan, for example," says CNN business writer Katie Lobosco, "while competitors' products from countries participating in the new [TPP] will eventually be duty-free."[48]

In August 2018 Trump announced plans to withdraw the United States from the North American Free Trade Agreement (NAFTA). This deal had governed trade with Canada and Mexico since it was signed in 1993 by President Bill Clinton. Financial markets panicked at the potential disruption. However, Trump soon secured a new agreement with Mexico and Canada that kept many of NAFTA's features in place. He also declared victory on his main goal of lowering the United States' trade deficit (a condition in which the total value of a country's imports is greater than the total value of its exports). But few things ever get permanently settled in the Trump White House. By May 2019 the president was threatening to slap new tariffs on Mexican goods due to the border dispute, a move that was called off only when the Mexican government agreed to increase its own efforts at border control.

Using Tariffs as Punishment

In place of wide-ranging trade pacts that he obviously distrusts, Trump prefers what he calls the art of deal making. He believes in his ability to extract more favorable terms when negotiating with other nations one-on-one. He insists that his predecessors too often settled for deals that did not benefit American farmers and factory workers. Moreover, Trump does not shy away from hardball tactics. He shrugs if a deal falls through and always seems prepared to walk away. He has boasted that trade wars are easy to win. He is comfortable using threats, especially the threat of tariffs. If negotiations call for both a carrot and a stick—with the carrot as an incentive, the stick as a threat—tariffs are the stick Trump relies on to punish trading partners.

For instance, following the US pullout from the TPP, Trump turned his attention to the United States' trade relations with China. Trump made clear his concerns about China stealing American technology and breaking promises to open its markets. In talks with Chinese president Xi Jinping and Xi's trade advisers, Trump repeatedly threatened to raise tariffs on Chinese products. He showed his hand first in February 2018 by placing tariffs on solar panels and washing machines manufactured in several different countries, including China. In September 2018 Trump slapped

Chinese factory workers make photovoltaic cells for solar panels. Fears of an all-out trade war grew in 2018 and 2019 after Trump placed tariffs on Chinese-made goods and China retaliated by doing the same with American products.

tariffs on more than $200 billion of Chinese goods. The tariff rates started at 10 percent, with increases up to 25 percent. One day later Xi responded by announcing new tariffs on $60 billion worth of American goods. He also canceled trade talks with Trump's team, signaling what many feared was the start of a trade war.

Yet negotiations resumed in 2019, initially in Beijing and later in Washington, DC. Treasury secretary Steven Mnuchin and US

Large Cost of Steel Tariffs

Trump's use of tariffs to support certain American businesses inevitably creates winners and losers. For example, he took office promising to revive the United States steel and aluminum industry. He accused China and other nations of dumping surplus steel on the American market, causing prices to plummet. A US Department of Commerce report highlighted several steel mill closures in recent years, along with the loss of several thousand jobs. In retaliation, Trump announced large new tariffs—25 percent on steel and 10 percent on aluminum. At rallies in Pennsylvania, the top steel-producing state, Trump vowed to help steel companies compete and in turn raise workers' wages. Many Democrats quietly approved of the action, having urged passage of steel tariffs for years.

Trump's move did bolster the American steel industry but at large cost to the overall American economy. Manufacturers of everything from automobiles to safety pins suddenly faced a jump in steel prices. Some coped by passing on the added cost to customers or substituting other materials for the steel in their products. The Peterson Institute, a nonprofit research center for international economic policy, estimates that Trump's steel and aluminum tariffs have cost the US economy about $11.5 billion a year. Each steelworker's job saved cost US consumers about $900,000. As economic reporters Eduardo Porter and Guilbert Gates contend, "The lesson the White House has yet to figure out is that the tariffs meant to protect the businesses that make these metals will end up hamstringing the industries that rely on them."

Eduardo Porter and Guilbert Gates, "How Trump's Protectionism Could Backfire," *New York Times*, March 20, 2018. www.nytimes.com.

trade representative Robert Lighthizer met with Chinese vice premier Liu He, with the two sides edging toward a breakthrough agreement. Trump was so confident that he invited Xi to his Florida estate at Mar-a-Lago to nail down the details. However, just when a deal seemed in reach, Trump changed his mind once more. He accused the Chinese of seeking to renegotiate matters that had already been settled. Trump restored the previous tariffs on Chinese goods and threatened more tariffs on $325 billion worth of Chinese products. China reacted with new tariffs on $110 billion worth of US goods. World financial markets wobbled at the prospect of an all-out US-China trade war. Observers in the United States feared that Trump's swaggering approach would backfire this time. As conservative economic advocates Grover Norquist and Timothy Phillips note, "While we certainly have legitimate concerns about abusive Chinese trade practices, including the theft of our intellectual property, these issues should be dealt with through international institutions such as the World Trade Organization, where the United States wins 85 percent of the cases it brings. This work requires a scalpel, but tariffs are a club."[49]

> "This work [of trade negotiation] requires a scalpel, but tariffs are a club."[49]
>
> —Conservative advocates Grover Norquist and Timothy Phillips

Jobs, Growth, but Also Uncertainty

Under Trump the US economy has performed well, with continuing growth in GDP, jobs, and wages. His tax cuts and deregulation policies have mostly been effective in helping American businesses compete in the global marketplace. He has scrapped old multinational trade agreements in a quest for better terms for American interests. At the same time, Trump's willingness to confront trading partners such as China and the European Union with threats of tariffs has spread anxiety in world markets. As Jack Nasher, an expert in negotiation strategy, notes, "US President Donald Trump's negotiation style has been consistent throughout his real estate career and his presidency: anything goes."[50]

CHAPTER FIVE

Controversy on the Environment

In mid-January 2019 the US Department of Defense released a new report on the threat of climate change. The report described how dozens of US military bases are under threat from climate-related conditions, including drought, wildfire, and rising seas. It also detailed how military missions and operational plans could be affected by disruptive climate effects. In essence, the Pentagon was confirming that it believes climate change is a threat to national security.

A few days later, Trump tweeted about the frigid winter weather: "In the beautiful Midwest, windchill temperatures are reaching minus 60 degrees, the coldest ever recorded. In coming days, expected to get even colder. People can't last outside even for minutes. What the hell is going on with Global Warming? Please come back fast, we need you!"[51] The tweet was typical for Trump, making light of climate change and setting environmentalists' teeth on edge. When viewed next to the Pentagon report, Trump's message also reveals the divisions in his administration and in his own political party. During the 2016 presidential campaign, he referred to climate change as a Chinese hoax. In 2017 Trump removed climate change from the list of national security threats. Yet growing numbers of young Trump supporters have problems with the president's stance. "There's disagreement there with Donald Trump," says Tex Fischer, a twenty-two-year-old Ohio conservative. "I don't personally know anyone involved in young, right-of-center politics that doesn't believe climate change is an issue. . . . Conservatives that care about the environment do exist."[52]

Pulling Out of the Paris Climate Agreement

The environment is one more area in which Trump has sought to reverse Obama's policies. Trump's skepticism about climate change led him to make a tone-setting move early in his presidency. On June 1, 2017, Trump announced that the United States was withdrawing from the Paris climate agreement. The Paris pact is a historic attempt to marshal the world community to take action against mounting levels of carbon dioxide (CO_2) in the atmosphere and rising temperatures. It was originally signed in 2015 by 174 nations plus the European Union. The United States and China, which together account for 40 percent of global CO_2 emissions, agreed to sign in 2016.

Trump resisted an intense lobbying effort by Democrats, corporate leaders, certain cabinet officials such as Secretary of State Rex Tillerson (a former ExxonMobil chair and CEO), and members of his own family, including his daughter Ivanka. In the end, he agreed with advisers such as Scott Pruitt, then-head of the US Environmental Protection Agency (EPA), that the agreement was bad for America. By pulling out, Trump was keeping one of his first and most often repeated campaign promises.

In remarks delivered in the White House Rose Garden, the president said he was committed to protecting the environment. And he claimed to be willing to negotiate a better agreement that did not seek to punish the United States. But he also stressed his policy of America First. Although the Paris agreement allowed each nation to set its own rules, Trump claimed it was an effort

> "I don't personally know anyone involved in young, right-of-center politics that doesn't believe climate change is an issue. . . . Conservatives that care about the environment do exist."[52]
>
> —Tex Fischer, a twenty-two-year-old Ohio conservative

> "I was elected to represent the citizens of Pittsburgh, not Paris."[53]
>
> —Trump announcing his decision to pull out of the Paris climate agreement on June 1, 2017

by international groups to dictate environmental rules for the United States. He said he refused to let this happen. As Trump explained, "I was elected to represent the citizens of Pittsburgh, not Paris."[53]

Trump's rejection of the Paris pact drew criticism from politicians, business leaders, scientists, and academics in many countries. As the world's number two (after China) emitter of CO_2, the United States' participation was considered essential for the agreement to succeed. Democrats realized that Trump had no intention of reversing course, no matter the consequences. "Removing the United States from the Paris agreement is a reckless and indefensible action," said Al Gore, former vice president and a leading voice for fighting climate change. "It undermines America's standing in the world and threatens to damage humanity's ability to solve the climate crisis in time."[54] Today the United States is the only nation in the world still rejecting the Paris agreement. Under its terms, the United States cannot officially withdraw until 2020.

Dumping the Clean Power Plan

In October 2017 Trump rolled back another piece of Obama's environmental legacy, the Clean Power Plan. The plan was designed to curb carbon emissions from America's power plants. For the first time it set emissions goals for each state, allowing the states to work out their own means of reaching the goals. The plan's overall objective was to cut emissions in the United States by more than 30 percent below 2005 levels. Although the Supreme Court ruled that control of CO_2 emissions was a legitimate aim of the EPA, legal challenges by several states had kept the plan from being fully implemented.

Coal-fired power plants were special targets of the Obama plan. In order to meet new emissions and environmental standards, coal-fired plants had to be fitted with expensive new technologies. New regulations for treating wastewater from coal plants cost operators more than $2.5 billion. At the same time, cheap and abundant natural gas replaced coal-based power plants in many communities. Falling prices for renewable energy projects also put pressure on coal. States from Alabama to Pennsylvania retired old coal-fired generators that no longer made economic sense.

In dumping the Clean Power Plan, Trump sought to give states even more flexibility in how they address carbon emissions. Another goal was to support the coal industry and mining workers, as Trump had promised to do in his campaign. Yet coal-plant closings actually doubled in the first two years of the Trump administration. According to a report by the Institute for Energy Economics and Financial Analysis, a record amount of

Shortly after the US Department of Defense issued a report on the national security threat posed by climate change, Trump tweeted about the Midwest's frigid winter weather and wondered what had happened to global warming.

coal-fired power capacity was retired in 2018. With alternate energy sources becoming as cheap or cheaper than coal, the trend is expected to continue through 2024.

The Trump EPA's replacement for the Clean Power Plan, called the Affordable Clean Energy rule, seems unlikely to restore coal's place in America's power generation. And experts on the environment doubt whether the new rule is even intended to reduce carbon emissions. The *Washington Post* claims that the new EPA rule would allow twelve times more carbon emissions than Obama's Clean Power Plan would have. David Konisky, an associate professor at Indiana University's School of Public and Environmental Affairs, agrees that the rule lacks teeth. "I think this is a rule designed to technically comply with the obligation the EPA is under to regulate CO_2 without actually being a serious policy effort,"[55] he says.

> "I think this is a rule designed to technically comply with the obligation the EPA is under to regulate CO_2 without actually being a serious policy effort."[55]
>
> —David Konisky, associate professor at Indiana University's School of Public and Environmental Affairs, on Trump's Affordable Clean Energy rule

Controversy over Reductions in Greenhouse Gases

The increasing number of coal-plant shutdowns under Trump helps support one of the administration's most controversial claims. In October 2018, EPA director Andrew Wheeler (who replaced Pruitt) released data showing that total emissions of CO_2—one of the greenhouse gases—dropped 2.7 percent from 2016 to 2017. Wheeler credited Trump's reform agenda for environmental regulations for the drop. He also noted that many nations that joined the Paris climate agreement could not match the US record on emissions reductions. "While many around the world are talking about reducing greenhouse gases, the U.S. continues to deliver," said Wheeler, "and today's report is further evidence of our action-oriented approach."[56]

Wheeler's claim made environmentalists roll their eyes. They pointed out that the plunge in emissions began under the Obama

Trump has reversed many of the environmental policies of his predecessor, President Barack Obama. One of these policies is the Clean Power Plan, which sought to curb carbon emissions from coal-fired power plants (pictured).

administration due to its new regulations and shutdowns of coal-fired power plants. "This is both political plagiarism [stealing] and vandalism," says David Doniger, senior strategic director at the Natural Resources Defense Council. "Trump's EPA appointees are claiming credit for their predecessors' work and trying to destroy it at the same time."[57]

Most environmentalists expect emissions numbers to begin rising as a result of Trump's energy policies. Indeed, figures for 2018 showed a sharp rise of about 3 percent in CO_2 emissions in the United States, the first such rise in four years. The jump in the power sector alone was 1.9 percent. Trump's program of assuring plenty of reliable power while also holding emissions in check may be faltering.

Support for Fracking

Trump has also promoted a new age of energy production in America. As coal-fired plants are shuttered, they are often replaced not by solar or wind but by cheap natural gas. The revolution in oil and

Disdain for Renewable Energy

At the Conservative Political Action Conference on March 2, 2019, Trump took delight in mocking the so-called Green New Deal proposed by a group of congressional Democrats. He took special aim at the idea of replacing fossil fuels with renewable energy sources for power generation. "When the wind stops blowing, that's the end of your electric," he told the audience. "Let's hurry up. 'Darling, is the wind blowing today? I'd like to watch television, darling.'"

Trump's disdain for renewables, including wind and solar power, is reflected in his budget proposals for 2020. He wants to slash funding for research on energy efficiency and renewable energy at several national labs. Funding for wind projects would be cut by two-thirds. As for Trump's riff on the problems with wind energy, environmental experts say the president is only partly correct. Power systems that rely on wind turbines are fed by winds along a vast network, not just in the user's backyard. As Michael Gillenwater, executive director of the Greenhouse Gas Management Institute, observes, "Just because the wind stops blowing in one place does not mean the whole grid goes down." However, wind power is indeed intermittent—as Trump says, winds are unpredictable—and without battery technology to store wind-generated power, fossil fuel sources are still needed to fill the gaps.

Quoted in John Kruzel, "Fact-Checking Donald Trump's Take on Wind Energy," PolitiFact, April 3, 2019. www.politifact.com.

---

gas development in the United States, begun during the Obama years, has made America the world's leading energy producer. Whereas not long ago the United States depended in large part on foreign sources of oil, it now is close to being a net exporter of oil and natural gas—selling more fossil fuels on the world market than it buys.

The key to this revolution is a process called hydraulic fracturing, or fracking for short. It fractures underground rock formations to release oil and gas deposits trapped within. Under Trump, fracking has seen a huge increase on federal lands, including in Wyoming and large expanses in the West. Reversing Obama-era policies, Trump's Department of the Interior has auctioned off drilling rights to millions of acres of public lands. In fiscal year 2018 alone, more than 12.8 million acres went up for lease, which was triple the number in Obama's entire second term. With energy prices on the rise, oil and gas developers see the Trump policy as a bonanza.

The Trump administration's rollback of regulations also has played a part in the fracking boom. Oil and gas lobbyists have won favorable changes in rules on land use, leases of public lands, approval of drilling permits, and royalty payments. Restrictions on access to endangered wildlife habitats have been eased. The amount of time for the public to protest drilling leases has also been reduced. "The president, love him or hate him, he's doing what he said he would do in Washington," observes Samantha McDonald, formerly a top lobbyist at the Independent Petroleum Association of America. "He's been actively pursuing a deregulatory agenda that has had millions of dollars of impact."[58]

Environmentalists view Trump's pro-fracking policies as an ongoing disaster for the land, wildlife, the atmosphere, and the climate. A proposal by the Bureau of Land Management to allow fracking activity in eight central California counties has been labeled dangerous due to nearby fault zones and has drawn widespread protests. "Our concern is that the Trump administration is planning to open up California to fracking and dangerous drilling at all," says Clare Lakewood, senior attorney at the Climate Law Institute at the Center for Biological Diversity. "We know that Californians don't want it. And yet we see they're pushing this through."[59]

> "Our concern is that the Trump administration is planning to open up California to fracking and dangerous drilling at all. We know that Californians don't want it. And yet we see they're pushing this through."[59]
>
> —Clare Lakewood, senior attorney at the Climate Law Institute at the Center for Biological Diversity

Rethinking Fuel Economy Standards

Federal rules on fuel economy in automobiles have also been eased under Trump. In August 2018, after two years of talks with auto industry heads, the US Department of Transportation and EPA announced a freeze on fuel economy standards, or how many miles per gallon (mpg) a vehicle gets. This altered Obama's 2012 plan to attain an average fuel economy of 54.5 mpg (23.2 km/L) by 2025 for each company's fleet of vehicles. Under the new rules, cars would only have to average about 37 mpg (15.7 km/L) by 2025. As Wheeler, the head of the EPA, remarked in a press release, "More realistic standards can save lives while continuing to improve the environment. We value the public's input as we engage in this process in an open, transparent manner."[60] Trump's EPA tried to arrange for a fifty-state solution that would bar individual states from setting their own, stricter standards.

Experts worry that the Trump administration's plans to roll back federal fuel economy standards could slow the adoption of electric cars. Electric cars, such as those pictured, produce less air pollution than gasoline models.

Ending Protections for the Gray Wolf

The Trump administration's emphasis on oil drilling, mining, and ranching interests has affected endangered species in many areas of the nation. In March 2019, for example, the US Fish and Wildlife Service (FWS) sought to remove the gray wolf from federal protection in the lower forty-eight states. David Bernhardt, acting secretary of the interior and a former oil lobbyist, said the move showed the success of FWS policies. "The facts are clear and indisputable—the gray wolf no longer meets the definition of a threatened or endangered species," said Bernhardt. "Today the wolf is thriving on its vast range, and it is reasonable to conclude it will continue to do so in the future."

From a low of one thousand in 1975, the gray wolf population now numbers almost six thousand. Nonetheless, environmentalists urge that it is much too soon to lift the endangered species protections for the gray wolf. They point out that farmers and ranchers consider gray wolves a threat and a nuisance. Without federal limits, they are likely to hunt the wolves aggressively. Collette Adkins, a senior attorney at the Center for Biological Diversity, fears that the Trump administration is more interested in politics than wildlife protection. "We know from experience that states can't be trusted to sustainably manage wolves," says Adkins. "When they lose their federal protections, they get subjected to aggressive trophy hunting, trapping, killing at the behest of the agricultural [livestock] industry."

Quoted in Jacob Shea, "Trump Administration Wants More Wolves Off Endangered Species List," *Sierra*, April 11, 2019. www.sierraclub.org.

However, fourteen states, including California, have sued the White House to maintain control over their state standards.

In June 2019 seventeen automakers sent a letter to the White House protesting the lower standards for fuel economy. They fear that the new plan will spur environmentally conscious states into setting their own standards, forcing automobile companies to spend more in tailoring their vehicles to different states and regions. The automakers urged Trump to settle on a compromise in fuel economy standards halfway between the Obama plan and the new proposal. However, several states, including California, have rejected all talk of compromise on fuel economy standards, and the administration seems unlikely to change its proposed plan. In addition, experts said the new rules threatened to slow the adoption of electric cars, which produce less pollution than gasoline models. To environmentalists, the new rules were once more taking the United States in the wrong direction.

Trump's approach to the environment is marked by skepticism about the role of humans in climate change and a drive to undo the previous administration's environmental policies. Trump has withdrawn the United States from the Paris climate agreement, isolating the United States as a holdout, and he has scrapped Obama's Clean Power Plan. Although CO_2 emissions initially fell during Trump's administration, later reports show emissions increasing. Trump's agencies have also relaxed rules to allow more drilling for oil and natural gas on federal lands, including fracking. He has lowered targets for fuel economy despite the protests of several states and many major automakers. Trump believes his approach is based on common sense, as opposed to the radical policies of the left. But time and again he has favored business interests over environmental concerns. It remains to be seen whether Trump's environmental record will cost him support among independents and even some conservative voters in his bid for reelection in 2020.

SOURCE NOTES

Introduction: A President Like No Other

1. Quoted in John Fritze and Christal Hayes, "Trump Says 'Strongly Looking' at Plan to Send Immigrants to Sanctuary Cities," *USA Today*, April 12, 2019. www.usatoday.com.
2. Paul Krugman, "The Economic Fallout," *New York Times*, November 9, 2016. www.nytimes.com.
3. Quoted in Kevin Breuninger, "Trump Slams the Media as 'the True Enemy of the People' Days After CNN Was Targeted with Mail Bombs," CNBC, October 29, 2018. www.cnbc.com.
4. Quoted in Gary Younge, "'Trump Hasn't Just Done a Good Job, He's Done a Great Job,'—the View from Muncie, Indiana," *Guardian* (Manchester), January 22, 2018. www.theguardian.com.

Chapter One: A Combative Style

5. Quoted in Brian Naylor, "Trump Lashes Out During Combative Press Conference," NPR, November 7, 2018. www.npr.org.
6. Quoted in Naylor, "Trump Lashes Out During Combative Press Conference."
7. Quoted in Tom Lutey, "Trump: 'We're Going to Win So Much, You're Going to Be So Sick and Tired of Winning,'" *Billings (MT) Gazette*, May 26, 2016. www.billingsgazette.com.
8. Quoted in Chris Cillizza, "The Awful Reality That Donald Trump's Repeated Attacks on John McCain Prove," CNN, March 19, 2019. www.cnn.com.
9. Cillizza, "The Awful Reality That Donald Trump's Repeated Attacks on John McCain Prove."
10. Quoted in Lauren Johnson, "Trump Calls Conservative Pundit Ann Coulter a 'Wacky Nut Job' Ahead of Speech Near Mar-a-Lago," Business Insider, March 10, 2019. www.businessinsider.com.

11. Peter Baker, "Victor or Victim? Trump's Changing Response to Mueller Report," *New York Times*, April 24, 2019. www.nytimes.com.
12. Quoted in Politico, "Trump's Twitter Year of Outrage and Braggadocio," December 31, 2018. www.politico.com.
13. Quoted in "Trump's Twitter Year of Outrage and Braggadocio," *Politico*, December 31, 2018. www.politico.com.
14. Matt Taibbi, "The Press Will Learn Nothing from the Russiagate Fiasco," *Rolling Stone*, April 23, 2019. www.rollingstone.com.
15. Quoted in Brian Bennett, "'This Is Very Good.' How Trump Beat the Mueller Investigation," *Time*, March 28, 2019. www.time.com.
16. Quoted in Cheyenne Haslett, "Former White House Aide Cliff Sims Describes 'Team of Vipers' Under Trump in Interview on New Book," ABC News, January 28, 2019. www.abcnews.go.com.
17. Olivia Nuzzi, "How Donald Trump Decides to Fire Someone," *New York*, June 30, 2017. www.nymag.com.

Chapter Two: Reversing Course in Foreign Policy

18. Quoted in Peter Baker, "Viktor Orban, Hungary's Far-Right Leader, Gets Warm Welcome from Trump," *New York Times*, May 13, 2019. www.nytimes.com.
19. Michael Anton, "The Trump Doctrine," *Foreign Policy*, April 20, 2019. www.foreignpolicy.com.
20. Quoted in Niall Stanage, "The Memo: Trump Puts Isolationism at Center Stage," *Hill* (Washington, DC), December 27, 2018. www.thehill.com.
21. Stacie L. Pettyjohn, "'Cost Plus 50' Explained," Rand Corporation, March 15, 2019. www.rand.org.
22. Quoted in Julian E. Barnes and Helene Cooper, "Trump Discussed Pulling U.S. from NATO, Aides Say amid New Concerns over Russia," *New York Times*, January 14, 2019. www.nytimes.com.
23. Quoted in Krishnadev Calamur, "Nine Notorious Dictators, Nine Shout-Outs from Donald Trump," *Atlantic*, March 4 2018. www.theatlantic.com.

24. Quoted in *New York Times*, "How Republican Lawmakers Responded to Trump's Russian Meddling Denial," July 17, 2018. www.nytimes.com.
25. Quoted in Council on Foreign Relations, "North Korean Nuclear Negotiations, 1985–2019," 2019. www.cfr.org.
26. Quoted in David Jackson, "Vietnam Summit: From Fire and Fury to Love Letters, Trump to Hold Second Meeting with North Korea's Kim," *USA Today*, February 26, 2019. www.usatoday.com.
27. Quoted in Youkyung Lee, "Trump and Kim's Cozy Relationship Makes Nuclear Talks Tougher," *Bloomberg Businessweek*, May 19, 2019. www.bloomberg.com.
28. Quoted in Adam Kredo, "Dem Leaders Side with Iran as Trump Admin Seeks to Counter Terror Regime," *Washington Free Beacon*, May 22, 2019. www.freebeacon.com.

Chapter Three: Illegal Immigration and Building the Wall

29. Quoted in Adam Shaw, "Trump Visits Southern Border amid Growing Crisis, Declaring That 'Our Country Is Full,'" Fox News, May 13, 2019. www.foxnews.com.
30. Quoted in Shaw, "Trump Visits Southern Border amid Growing Crisis, Declaring That 'Our Country Is Full.'"
31. Quoted in Ishaan Tharoor, "Trump Says Borders Make a Country. But There's a Lot More to It," *Washington Post*, August 1, 2018. www.washingtonpost.com.
32. Quoted in John Burnett, "Borderland Trump Supporters Welcome a Wall in Their Own Backyard," NPR, August 12, 2016. www.npr.org.
33. Quoted in *Time*, "Here's Donald Trump's Presidential Announcement Speech," June 16, 2015. www.time.com.
34. Quoted in Ronald Brownstein, "Trump's Immigration Policies Unify White Republicans," *Atlantic*, April 11, 2019. www.theatlantic.com.
35. Quoted in William A. Galston, "As Trump's Zero-Tolerance Immigration Policy Backfires, Republicans Are in Jeopardy," Brookings Institution, June 18, 2018. www.brookings.edu.

36. Quoted in Galston, "As Trump's Zero-Tolerance Immigration Policy Backfires, Republicans Are in Jeopardy."
37. Quoted in Tatiana Sanchez, "'We Will Continue Fighting': DACA Recipients, TPS Holders Reject Trump Plan," *San Francisco Chronicle*, January 19, 2019. www.sfchronicle.com.
38. Sophia Lee, "Who's Funding the Migrant Caravans?," *World*, April 15, 2019. https://world.wng.org.
39. Quoted in Adam Shaw, "Obama's Border Chief Warns Congress: Immigration Crisis 'at a Magnitude Never Seen in Modern Times,'" Fox News, April 4, 2019. www.foxnews.com.

Chapter Four: Tax Cuts and Tariffs for the Economy

40. Quoted in Molly Schuetz and Edwin Chan, "Trump's Throttling of Huawei Could Backfire on U.S. Tech," Bloomberg, May 25, 2019. www.bloomberg.com.
41. Quoted in Jane C. Timm, "Fact Check: Did Trump Pull Off an 'Economic Turnaround?,'" NBC News, September 10, 2018. www.nbcnews.com.
42. Stephen Moore and Arthur Laffer, "It's Trump's Economy Now," *Wall Street Journal*, June 7, 2018. www.wsj.com.
43. Quoted in David Choi, "'Irresponsible, Reckless, Unjust, and Just Plain Cruel': Democrats Blast GOP Tax Bill After It Passes," Business Insider, December 20, 2017. www.businessinsider.com.
44. Quoted in Choi, "'Irresponsible, Reckless, Unjust, and Just Plain Cruel.'"
45. *Investor's Business Daily*, "Go Figure: Federal Revenues Hit All-Time Highs Under Trump Tax Cuts," October 16, 2018. www.investors.com.
46. Quoted in Binyamin Appelbaum and Jim Tankersley, "The Trump Effect: Business Anticipating Less Regulation, Loosens Purse Strings," *New York Times*, January 1, 2018. www.nytimes.com.
47. Sam Berger, "Commentary: How Trump Is Letting Businesses Steal Money from Workers," *Fortune*, January 31, 2018. www.fortune.com.
48. Katie Lobosco, "Trump Pulled Out of a Massive Trade Deal. Now 11 Countries Are Going Ahead Without the US," CNN, December 29, 2018. www.cnn.com.

49. Grover Norquist and Timothy Phillips, "Why Trade War with China Is a Dangerous Game for America," *Hill* (Washington, DC), May 21, 2019. www.thehill.com.
50. Jack Nasher, "Trump's Gamble: How Hardball Negotiation Tactics Can Win the U.S.-China Trade War," *Forbes*, May 27, 2019. www.forbes.com.

Chapter Five: Controversy on the Environment

51. Quoted in Kendra Pierre-Louis, "Why Is the Cold Weather So Extreme If the Earth Is Warming?," *New York Times*, January 31, 2019. www.nytimes.com.
52. Quoted in Oliver Milman, "Millennial Trump Supporters Are Breaking with Their Party over Climate Change," *Mother Jones*, April 15, 2019. www.motherjones.com.
53. Quoted in Michael D. Shear, "Trump Will Withdraw U.S. from Paris Climate Agreement," *New York Times*, June 1, 2017. www.nytimes.com.
54. Quoted in Shear, "Trump Will Withdraw U.S. from Paris Climate Agreement."
55. Quoted in Tom DiChristopher, "Trump Administration to Replace Obama's Clean Power Plan with Weaker Greenhouse Gas Rules for Power Plants," CNBC, August 21, 2018. www.cnbc.com.
56. Quoted in Jennifer A. Dlouhy and Eric Roston, "Trump EPA Draws Scorn for Touting Lower Greenhouse-Gas Emissions," Bloomberg, October 17, 2018. www.bloomberg.com.
57. Quoted in Dlouhy and Roston, "Trump EPA Draws Scorn for Touting Lower Greenhouse-Gas Emissions."
58. Quoted in Eric Lipton and Hiroko Tabuchi, "Driven by Trump Policy Changes, Fracking Booms on Public Lands," *New York Times*, October 27, 2018. www.nytimes.com.
59. Quoted in Jeff Daniels, "Trump Administration's California Fracking Plan Is 'Dangerous,' Environmental Groups Say," CNBC, May 3, 2019. www.cnbc.com.
60. Quoted in "U.S. EPA and DOT Propose Fuel Economy Standards for MY 2021–2016 Vehicles," US Environmental Protection Agency, August 2, 2018. www.epa.gov.

FOR FURTHER RESEARCH

Books

Francisco Cantú, *The Line Becomes a River: Dispatches from the Border*. New York: Riverhead, 2018.

Victor Davis Hanson, *The Case for Trump*. New York: Basic Books, 2019.

Dominick Reston, *Donald Trump: 45th US President*. San Diego: ReferencePoint, 2018.

Cliff Sims, *Team of Vipers: My 500 Extraordinary Days in the Trump White House*. New York: Thomas Dunne, 2019.

Donald J. Trump and Tony Schwartz, *Trump: The Art of the Deal*. New York: Ballantine, 2015.

Michael Wolff, *Fire and Fury: Inside the Trump White House*. New York: Holt, 2018.

Bob Woodward, *Fear: Trump in the White House*. New York: Simon & Schuster, 2018.

Internet Sources

Peter Baker and Maggie Haberman, "Trump Undercuts Bolton on North Korea and Iran," *New York Times*, May 28, 2019. www.nytimes.com.

Ted Hesson, "Here's What's Driving the 'Crisis' at the Border," Politico, March 28, 2019. www.politico.com.

Ben Leubsdorf, "Economists Credit Trump as Tailwind for U.S. Growth, Hiring and Stocks," *Wall Street Journal*, January 11, 2018. wsj.com.

Domenico Montanaro, "6 Strongmen Trump Has Praised—and the Conflicts It Presents," NPR, May 2, 2017. www.npr.org.

Lucy Rodgers and Dominic Bailey, "Trump Wall—All You Need to Know About US Border in Seven Charts," BBC, May 31, 2019. www.bbc.com.

Jim Tankersley, "Trump Owns the Economy Now, for Better or Worse," *New York Times*, March 28, 2019. www.nytimes.com.

Websites

Donald J. Trump for President (www.donaldjtrump.com). This website for the 2020 presidential campaign presents a brief biography of President Trump, a list of campaign promises along with reports on Trump's efforts to keep them, news and updates about Trump, and a schedule of campaign rallies and fund-raising events.

Donald J. Trump/The White House (www.whitehouse.gov). The official White House website features biographical and other information about the president and members of his administration. The site also includes speeches and policy memoranda on such issues as the economy, national security, the federal budget, immigration, and the opioid crisis.

Politifact: Donald Trump's File (www.politifact.com/personalities/donald-trump). This website maintains a scorecard on the veracity of Trump's remarks in speeches, interviews, and tweets. His words are analyzed and given ratings of True, Mostly True, Half True, Mostly False, False, and Pants on Fire. The site also checks the truthfulness of comments about Trump and his administration.

US Department of Justice (www.justice.gov/storage/report.pdf). Volumes I and II of the "Report on the Investigation into Russian Interference in the 2016 Presidential Election" by Special Counsel Robert S. Mueller III can be found here. The redacted report, released in March 2019 by the special counsel's office, appears in full. Related court documents, including indictments and plea agreements stemming from the investigation, can be found at www.justice.gov/sco.

INDEX

Note: Boldface page numbers indicate illustrations.

ABC News/*Washington Post* opinion poll, 35
Adkins, Collette, 65
Affordable Clean Energy rule, 60
America First
   economy and, 45, 51
   environment and, 57–58
   foreign affairs and, 21–22
American values, 10, 33
Antifa (antifascist) groups, 12
anti-Semitism, 12, 25
Apprentice, The (television program), 5, 18
approval rating, 13
art of deal making, 52–53
authoritarian leaders
   Trump's behavior compared to that of, 19
   Trump's friendly behavior toward, 20, **21**, 24–26, **26**
   Trump's ideas about, 25
automakers and fuel economy standards, 65–66

Baker, Peter, 11
Baker, Ted, 7
Berger, Sam, 51
Bernhardt, David, 65
Bernstein, Jared, 50
Biden, Joe, 12
Bin Salman, Mohammed, 25
Bolton, John, 30
Booker, Cory, 48
Brennan, John, 26
Bush, George W., 20, 37

Cabinet turnover
   firing of Tillerson and, 13, 18
   rate of, 17
   reasons for, 7, 18
Calexico, California, 32
California, 65, 66
Canada, 52
carbon dioxide (CO_2) emissions, 57, 58, 60–61
"Challenge Trump Poses to Objectivity, The" (Rutenberg in *New York Times*), 19
Charlottesville, Virginia, 12
Chávez, Hugo, 29
chief of staff turnover, 18
China
   accused of dumping steel, 54
   American companies prohibited from selling tech products to, 44–45
   global trade and, 52, **53**
   Paris climate agreement, 57
   tariffs imposed on, 53–55
   Xi Jinping as president for life of, 25
Chun Yung-woo, 28
Cillizza, Chris, 9–10
Clean Power Plan, 58–60
climate change, 56
Clinton, Bill, 52
Clinton, Hillary, 5–6
CNN opinion poll, 47
coal-fired power plants, 58–60, **61**
Comey, James, 15
Conservative Political Action Conference, 62
consumer protection, deregulation endangers, 51
Cost Plus 50 plan, 23–24
Coulter, Ann, 10
Cruz, Ted, 5
Cuba, 29

Deferred Action for Childhood Arrivals (DACA), 39

"Democracy Dies in Darkness"
  (Washington Post), 19
Democrats
  Bill Clinton, NAFTA, and 52
  Hillary Clinton campaign and, 5–6
  2018 midterm elections and, 8
  name-calling by Trump of, 10
  Trump slogan as jab at, 9
  See also Obama, Barack
Dempsey, Maria Guadalupe, 33
deregulation, 49–51, 63
dictators. *See* authoritarian leaders
Doniger, David, 61
Dreamers, 38–39
Durbin, Dick, 31

economy
  America First policy and, 45, 51
  budget deficit and, 48
  campaign promises about, 9
  government regulations on business and investment and, 49–51, 63
  gross domestic product and, 45, 48
  sales to Chinese tech companies and, 44–45
  steel and aluminum industry and, 54
  strength of, 7, 45
  tax reform and, 47–48
  trade agreements and, 51–52
  uncertainty about, 55
  See also tariffs
election(s)
  2016 presidential
    Clinton predicted as winner of, 5
    results, 6, 12
    Russian interference in, 15, 26, **26**
  2018 midterm, 8, 25, 50
  See also Trump presidential campaign
El Salvador, 41
employment
  black and Hispanic, 48
  job fairs, **49**
  levels, 45, 50
endangered species, 65
environment
  Affordable Clean Energy rule and, 60
  America First on Paris climate agreement and, 57–58
  climate change's threat to military and, 56
  CO_2 emissions and, 58–60
  deregulation endangers, 51, 63
  fracking and, 62–63
  fuel economy standards and, **64,** 64–66
  Green New Deal for, 62
  Trump denial of climate change and effects on, 56
  wildlife habitats and, 63
Erdogan, Recep Tayyip, 24
European Union, 24

"fake news," 7, 14
far-right groups, 12
FBI, on election of 2016, 15
Fischer, Tex, 56–57
Flake, Jeff, 26–27
Flournoy, Michéle A., 23, 24
Flynn, Michael, 15
foreign policy
  aid cut to El Salvador, Guatemala, and Honduras, 41
  America First as basis for, 21–22
  Cost Plus 50 plan, 23–24
  D-Day commemoration comments about, 23
  European leaders criticized and insulted by, 24
  Iran, 28–31, 38
  Iraq, 38
  Israel, 25
  NATO, 9, 22–23, 24
  North Korea, 27–28
  Orban and, 20
  overview of, 7
  "principled realism" approach of, 22
  Putin and, 26–27
  Saudi Arabia, 24–25, 38
  South Korea, 23, 28
  Trump promises about, during campaign, 9
  Venezuela, 29
fracking, 62–63
France, 23, 24
fuel economy standards, **64,** 64–66

Gates, Guilbert, 54
Gee, Dolly, 36
Germany, 23, 24
Gidley, Hogan, 17
Gillenwater, Michael, 62
Gleckman, Howard, 50

Golan Heights, 25
Gore, Al, 58
government shutdown, 39
gray wolf, 65
Green New Deal, 62
gross domestic product (GDP), 45, 48
Guaidó, Juan, 29
Guatemala, 41

Honduras, 41
Hu, Evanna, 45
Huawei, 44–45, **46**
Hungary, leader of, 20, **21**
hydraulic fracturing (fracking), 62–63

immigrants
  border wall and, **34**
    election campaign promise about, 33, 42
    government shutdown over, 39
    public opinion about, 35
    recently rebuilt, 32
  caravans of, **40,** 40–42
  core American values and, 33
  Dreamers as, 38–39
  increase in number and apprehensions of, 32
  Muslim ban on, 38
  racial bias and, 34
  sanctuary cities for, 4
  separation of, and families crossing border, **36,** 36–37
  threats to close border with Mexico over, 32
  Trump references to, during campaign, 9
  United States as full for, 32
  United States as nation of, 33
  zero-tolerance policy for, 35–37, **37**
Impeachment, 16
Institute for Energy Economics and Financial Analysis, 59–60
Investor's Business Daily, 48
Iran, 28–31, 38
Iraq, 38
Israel, 25

James, LeBron, 10
Jerusalem, 25

Kelly, John, 18

Khashoggi, Jamal, 24–25
Kim Jong Un, 27–28
Konisky, David, 60
Krugman, Paul, prediction after election of Trump, 6

Laffer, Arthur, 47
Lakewood, Clare, 63
Lee, Sophia, 41
Libya, 38
Lighthizer, Robert, 55
Liu He, 55
Lobosco, Katie, 52

Macron, Emmanuel, 23, 24
Maduro, Nicolás, 29
Make America Great Again (MAGA) slogan, 5, 8–9
May, Theresa, 23, 24
McCain, John, 9–10
McDonald, Samantha, 63
Merkel, Angela, 24
Mexico
  North American Free Trade Agreement and, 52
  payment for border wall by, 33, 42
  people coming from, 34
  threats to close border with, 32
  threats to impose tariffs on, 42, 52
military
  Iran and, 30
  NATO, 24
  "principled realism" and, 22
  strikes against terrorist groups, 7
  threats to, from climate change, 56
  Venezuela and, 29
Mnuchin, Steven, 54–55
Moore, Stephen, 47
Morgan, Mark, 41–42
Mueller, Robert, investigation by, 14–17, **14**
Mulvaney, Mick, 18
Muslims, ban on travel to United States, 38

Nasher, Jack, 55
nationalism, 21–22
NATO, 22–23, 24
natural gas, 61–62
neo-Nazis, 12

Netanyahu, Benjamin, 25
news media
    attacks on
        "fake news," 7, 14
        New York Times as failing enterprise, 10
        as "true Enemy of the People," 7
    changing standards of, 19
New York Post (newspaper), 36
New York Times (newspaper), 6, 10, 19
Nielsen, Kirstjen, 42–43
Norquist, Grover, 55
North American Free Trade Agreement (NAFTA), 52
North Atlantic Treaty Organization (NATO), 9, 22–23, 24
North Korea, 27–28
Notre Dame Cathedral fire (Paris), 14
nuclear weapons, 27–31
Nuzzi, Olivia, 18

Obama, Barack
    "catch and release" immigration policy of, 37
    Dreamers and, 39
    economy under, 46–47
    environmental program(s) of
        Clean Power Plan, 58–60
        CO_2 emissions reduction, 60–61
        fracking and, 63
        fuel economy standards for, 64
        Paris climate agreement and, 57
    nuclear agreement with Iran under, 28, 30
    Orban and, 20
    Trans-Pacific Partnership and, 51–52
    Trump campaign slogan as jab at, 9
    Twitter followers of, 13
Obrador, Andrés Manuel López, 42
oil drilling, 62, 65
oil tankers, 30, **31**
Orban, Viktor, 20, **21**

Palestinians, 25
Paris climate agreement, 57–58
Peña Nieto, Enrique, 42
personal privacy, deregulation endangers, 51
Peterson Institute, 54
Pettyjohn, Stacie L., 23–24

Pew Research Center, 25
Phillips, Timothy, 55
Politico, 14
Pompeo, Mike, 29, 30
Porter, Eduardo, 54
Priebus, Reince, 18
Prieto, Juan, 39
"principled realism" approach, 22
Pruitt, Scott, 57
public opinion
    of border wall, 35
    of economy under Trump, 47
    of government measures to prevent illegal entrance into United States, 35
    of tax reform, 47
    of Trump overall, 47
Pueblo sin Fronteras (City without Borders), 41
Putin, Vladimir, **26**
    election of 2016 and, 15, 26
    friendly with, 26–27
    Orban and, 20
    United States leaving NATO and, 24
    Venezuela and, 29

Quinnipiac opinion poll, 35

racial bias
    immigration policy and, 34–37, **37**
    Muslim ban and, 38
renewable energy, 62
Republican Party
    immigrants and, 35
    members not in administration, 18
    Trump trashing of, 5, 9–10
Rivlin, Douglas, 35
Roberts, John, 38
Rubio, Marco, 5
Russia. *See* Putin, Vladimir
Rutenberg, Jim, 19

sanctuary cities, 4, 33–34
Sanders, Bernie, 10, 48
Saudi Arabia, 24–25, 38
Seade, Jesus, 42
Sessions, Jeff, 35, 39
Sims, Cliff, 17
Somalia, 38
South Korea, 23, 28
Steele, Christopher, dossier by, 15, 16

Sudan, 38
Supreme Court, 7, 38, 58
Syria, 38

Taibbi, Matt, 16–17
tariffs
 cost of, to American economy, 54
 described, 45
 imposed on China, 53–55
 on steel and aluminum products, 54
 threats to impose, on Mexico, 42, 52
Tax Cuts and Jobs Act, 50
tax reform, 47–48
terrorism, 38
Tillerson, Rex, 13, 18, 57
trade agreements, 51–52
Trans-Pacific Partnership (TPP), 51–52
"true Enemy of the People," news media as, 7
Trump, Donald J., **6, 26**
 attacks made by
  against Mexican immigrants, 34
  against news media, 7, 8
  against other individuals, 5, 9, 10
 background, 4–5
 characteristics of
  belief in ability to make deals, 52–53
  bullying, 10
  combativeness, 8, 17, 18
  dislike of personal confrontation, 18
  impulsiveness, 17
  temperament, 7
  values loyalty over almost everything, 18
  winning as everything, 11
 false claims made by, 11, 12–13
 personal life, 5
Trump, Ivanka, 57
Trump, Melania, 36
Trump Organization, 4–5
Trump presidential campaign, **11**
 attacks on individuals, 5, 9–10
 attacks on US allies, 9
 on climate change as Chinese hoax, 56
 promises to build wall paid for by Mexico, 32–33, 42
 promises to lower taxes, 47
Trump Tower, 5
Trump University, 5
Turkey, 24

Twitter
 followers of Obama, 13
 followers of Trump, 13
 tweets by Trump
  about border control, 33
  about fighting Notre Dame Cathedral fire, 14
  about state of economy, 45
  about tariffs on products from Mexico in, 42
  attacks on Mueller investigation in, 15
  charges about media being "fake news" in, 14
  denial of existence of climate change in, 56, **59**
  firing of Secretary of State Tillerson in, 13, 18
  promises to stop using, 13
  threat to North Korean leader in, 27–28

Ukraine, 16, 27
Unite the Right rally (Charlottesville, Virginia), 12
United Kingdom, 23, 24
US Customs and Border Protection, 32, 41
US Department of Defense, 56
US Department of Health and Human Services (HHS), 36
US Department of Homeland Security (DHS), 36
US Department of Transportation, 64
US Environmental Protection Agency (EPA), 57, 64
US Fish and Wildlife Service (FWS), 65

Venezuela, 29

Warren, Elizabeth, 10
Washington Post (newspaper), 13, 19, 60
Wheeler, Andrew, 60, 64
white supremacist groups, 12
wildlife, endangered species, 65
wildlife habitats, 63

Xi Jinping, 25, 53, 55

Yemen, 38

zero-tolerance policy, 35–37, **37**

PICTURE CREDITS

Cover: Associated Press

6: Michael Candelori/Shutterstock.com
11: Associated Press
14: Associated Press
21: Associated Press
26: Associated Press
31: Associated Press
34: Karl_Sonnenberg/Shutterstock.com
37: Erin Scott/Zuma Press/Newscom
40: Jose Cabezas/Reuters/Newscom
46: iStockphoto.com
49: rblfmr/Shutterstock.com
53: Associated Press
59: natefishchpix/Shutterstock.com
61: PhilAugustavo/iStockphoto.com
64: iStockphoto.com

ABOUT THE AUTHOR

John Allen is a writer who lives in Oklahoma City.